Chani

His Ladies with the Lamps
Book 2

By

Ronna M. Bacon

ISBN 978-1-989699-95-9

The Ladies with the Lamps

Matthew 25: 6-10

6 "And at midnight a cry was heard: 'Behold, the bridegroom is coming; go out to meet him!' 7 Then all those virgins arose and trimmed their lamps. 8 And the foolish said to the wise, 'Give us some of your oil, for our lamps are going out.' 9 But the wise answered, saying, 'No, lest there should not be enough for us and you; but go rather to those who sell, and buy for yourselves.' 10 And while they went to buy, the bridegroom came, and those who were ready went in with him to the wedding; and the door was shut.

Chani

Isaiah 43:2

When you pass through the waters, I will be with you; And through the rivers, they shall not overflow you. When you walk through the fire you shall not be burned, nor shall the flame torch you.

NKJV

Table of Contents

Chapter 1
Chapter 2
Chapter 3
Chapter 4
Chapter 5
Chapter 6
Chapter 7
Chapter 8
Chapter 9
Chapter 10
Chapter 11
Chapter 12
Chapter 13
Chapter 14
Chapter 15
Chapter 16
Chapter 17
Chapter 18
Chapter 19
Chapter 20
Chapter 21
Chapter 22
Chapter 23
Chapter 24
Chapter 25
Chapter 26
Chapter 27
Chapter 28
Chapter 29
Chapter 30
Chapter 31

Chapter 32
Chapter 33
Chapter 34
Chapter 35
Chapter 36
Chapter 37
Chapter 38
Chapter 39
Chapter 40
Chapter 41
Chapter 42
Chapter 43
Chapter 44
Chapter 45
Epilogue
Dear Readers

Chapter 1

Waking in the middle of the night, Chani Whitman raised her head before she lowered it back to her pillow. She was on edge and had no idea why. It might have to do with what her cousin, Brinn, had just gone through, being abducted and then threatened by a local judge, but she doubted that. She had had a feeling for days now that she was under watch but couldn't see anyone.

Closing her eyes, she tried to resume her sleep but managed only to toss and turn. She squinted at the alarm clock. It was only five in the morning. She sighed. Today was to be rainy, and she hated rainy days. It meant that she would be stuck in her office, not out and about with her clients and working in their gardens. Her work as an ecological horticulturist was interesting and kept her out in the air during three seasons, working inside during the winter.

Chani rose at last, dressing and then heading for the kitchen, the kettle plugged in to make her tea, her cinnamon-raisin bagel in the toaster before she reached for her phone. Her sister, Eilis, had sent a text late the night before, asking if they could meet for a meal that day. She just needed her sister. Chani smiled, knowing how close that they all were, her sister, herself, and her two cousins. The four girls had lost their parents in what they had always believed to be an accident but that was now determined not to be the case. In fact, the investigators were looking at it as a murder. Their fathers' sister had taken them in, putting

—
7

aside her own plans and dreams to do that. Her fingers flew over the keyboard as she responded.

Heading for her office, Chani stared around the roads, seeing little traffic that morning. It surprised her. There was usually a lot more traffic than this, she thought. Her brown eyes searched the area before she shrugged. She pulled at the light brown hair that she had pulled back into a ponytail, not sure what the day would bring. Chani felt uneasy, shifting on her seat, feeling as if she was being watched.

"This is nonsense." Chani had a habit of talking aloud to herself. "There is no one there. What Brinn went through has got us all on edge. I just want to go away somewhere for a week or two and can't. Not at this time of year. Holidays are coming up soon, and then I will."

Pacing through the business where she worked, Chani frowned before checking her watch. It was unusual as well to find so few people in. In fact, no one other that she herself was in. It was a Friday, granted, but they were always busy trying to get their tasks done before the weekend. She dropped her backpack into her desk drawer and then headed for the kitchen, reaching to set the coffee that would be needed and plugging in the kettle. She hesitated and then unplugged it. Today, coffee was needed.

Hearing footsteps, Chani peeked out of the door, not recognizing the man who was approaching. She frowned before shaking her head. No, she thought, she didn't know him. But then, new people had been hired that very week, and maybe he was one of them.

"Can I help you?" She finally spoke, startling the man and causing him to spin and stare at her.

Ronan Rafferty sighed. This was not how this day was to start. He was jumping at nothing, he thought, and that was not the way to meet people. That was something he had trouble with, not liking to meet people. He preferred to be out on his farm, working away. Only, he had been asked to appear for a meeting that morning with the owner of the business. Just why that was, he had no idea. The owner, Jake Fraser, had not been specific, only stating that he needed some input from Ronan. Would his friend come and meet with him? Ronan had agreed reluctantly. He paused for a moment. *God, where are You? Are You here? I need that reassurance this morning,* he thought.

"I'm sorry. I was looking for Jake. He asked me to be here for a meeting this morning." Ronan hesitated to approach, shaking his head as the lady disappeared into the room. He stood just inside the doorway, the scent of freshly brewed coffee in his nostrils.

"Here, have some coffee." Chani pointed to the mug that she had poured. "I don't know how you like it." She grabbed her mug and moved away, apprehension in her movements for a moment.

Ronan ran a hand through his short-cropped black curls, his hazel eyes watchful. With his mug of coffee in his hand, he watched Chani.

"Aren't there usually more people here at this time? Jake seemed to imply that there would be."

—

9

"There should be. I don't understand that." Chani's phone was out as she scrolled through her messages. "Nothing from Jake. That's unusual. He's always here before anyone else."

Chani walked through the building, searching. It was as she thought. It was just herself and this man, this man named Ronan. She could hear his footsteps behind her as he followed her.

"My name's Ronan Rafferty." Ronan reached to halt her steps, his hand tightening on her arm for a moment.

"Hi. I'm Chani Whitman." Chani turned. "You go to the church I do. I've seen you there."

"I guess. Some Sundays I am away at a chapel I volunteer at. I wish that I had met you there." Ronan's hand tightened once more as he heard a soft sound. "Chani? Is there anyone in the back office?"

"No, there shouldn't be. It's not used on a regular basis." She was away before Ronan could stop her.

Ronan's head dropped, his eyes sliding closed. She just had to go and do that, didn't she? His rapid footsteps sounded after her, a hand on her arm stopping her once more.

Chani shot him a look before she moved to the doorway, staring at the room. Shocked at the mess, she didn't know where to start to clean it up.

Ronan stared past her, knowing that his friend would not have allowed such a mess to appear in any of his offices.

"Chani? What happened here?" Ronan watched her face, seeing a brief flicker of fear cross it. "Chani? What are you thinking?"

"I'm thinking that we're in trouble. We're not alone here." Chani spun, reaching for Ronan's hand and pulling him with her. "We need to find somewhere to hide." Her head was moving even as she ran for the back door, feeling Ronan's hand pulling back on her.

"Chani? I don't think we'll make it." Ronan slid to a stop, his action stopping Chani.

Chani swung, her mouth open to protest before it snapped closed. Her eyes widened at the sight of Ronan standing there with a gun muzzle tight to his temple. Her mouth opened and closed once more without a sound coming out.

We're in trouble, Lord. We need to get away and we can't. What do we do? Lord, I could really use an escape route right now. I thought we had an agreement. I don't want to go through an adventure like Brinn did.

Chapter 2

Chani stared at Ronan, finding his eyes steady on hers. She drew in a deep breath, somewhat reassured by his gaze. That was, until she raised her eyes to the gun. It was digging into his temple, and she could see that it was painful by the slight grimace that he made as the gun was pushed further at him.

"Who are you? Why are you in here? You're not allowed. You need to leave." Chani couldn't stop herself. It was not her nature to back down.

"Out. Out the back door. Now!" The man's bark caused her to jump and then dig in her heels not to move. "Now!"

Ronan sighed to himself before he reached out a hand, grasping Chani's hand and turning her towards the door.

"Chani? We need to go!" Ronan simply shook his head at her. "Please? We need to cooperate with this man."

"You do. I don't." Chani was obstinate in not moving, causing the man to shove her hard from behind. She stumbled forward, finding the door opening before she reached it. She drew in a deep breath. "This can't be really happening. God, we had an agreement. I wasn't to go through what Brinn did. Do You really mean this?"

Ronan frowned at her grumbling, not quite sure that he had heard her correctly. Was she really telling

God off? That was a new one for him. He certainly wouldn't be doing that.

Chani almost stomped towards the van, Ronan following closely behind her. He searched the area around them, looking for a way to escape. Only that didn't seem to be happening. He waited for the door to slide open, a hand out to help Chani into a seat and then seating himself. The man who had appeared sat beside him, the gun still in evidence.

Trying hard to control her fear, Chani thought back to what Brinn had been through. She had been abducted twice, Chani knew. Chani had wondered at the time how she had managed. It looked as if she was about to find out how to manage and survive this.

Ronan reached for her hand, his warm and strong on hers. He still searched for a way to escape. *This is not going good, Lord. How do we do this? How do I get free and take Chani with me? Or else get Chani free and back to her family? I don't see a way right yet.*

Chani clung to Ronan's hand before she stared at it. She did no*t* hold men's hands. Not ever! Yet here she was doing just that. She sighed to herself. *Now what? Where are we heading?* Her head turned as she stared out the side window. Chani frowned, seeing the section of town that they were heading to. This was not good.

Ronan watched Chani closely, seeing the distress and fear that she was hiding. What had he walked into, he wondered? It was definitely not what he had expected that morning. And he didn't think Jake had planned this. Where they were heading? That he had no idea. He just had to wait, he decided, and if an opportunity came up to get Chani away or send her away, he would do that.

Jake stood at the barricades on the street, a frown on his face. He had arrived at work, walking through the open building. He could see that Chani had been in. She was always one of the first there, but she wasn't there when he arrived. And Ronan's truck was in the parking lot, so he knew that his friend had arrived. He turned as he heard footsteps.

"Ashlynn? You're here?" He reached to hug the lady.

"I am. I am worried about Chani. She was to call me this morning and didn't. What's going on?" Ashlynn Whitman, Chani's aunt, had approached.

"I'm not sure. I arrived here and no one was in the building. The building was unlocked and the security system off. I know that Chani was here. So was a friend of mine who was to be here for a meeting." He looked around, trying to find answers. Only there were none.

"Oh, no! Please, Lord, not Chani!" Ashlynn grew distressed. She had had one niece undergo difficulty and danger and had been praying that the other three would escape that.

"We don't know that is what happened. The officers are going through there right now." Jake stuffed his hands into his jacket pockets. "This is not how the day was to start. Ashlynn? Where are the other girls?"

"At work, I hope. I'll have to call them." Her phone was out before she looked up to see a patrol officer approaching them. "Jake?"

"It's okay, Ashlynn. Hang tight. I'll be right back." Jake moved around the barrier and then towards the building. "What did you find?"

"The one office is tossed at the back. We don't know if anything is missing from there. That's something that you would be able to tell us. Other than that? No sign of them. We did find a backpack in the office where you said Chani works. We'll need you to tell us if it's hers."

Jake stared down into the desk drawer. Chani had been there after all. Her backpack was tucked away neatly, as it always was. She was a stickler for neatness, driving them crazy at times, but she always had a smile on her face as she insisted that they couldn't work in a mess. And she had been right, he had to acknowledge. He turned as he heard footsteps.

"Frank? You're here?" Jake reached to shake Frank's hand.

Frank, a detective on the force, nodded.

"I grabbed the call. Chani?"

Jake nodded in turn.

"Chani. She's missing. I know that she had arrived. And a friend of mine was here for a meeting." Jake moved away, heading for the back office, to stand and stare at the mess. "This is the only room that is disturbed. But they are nowhere in sight. And Ashlynn is at the barrier."

—

"I saw. Now, we need to talk. Any unhappy clients? Anyone trying to take over?" Frank watched Jake closely.

"No, not that I am aware of. Our people are well loved by their clients. They bring healing and happiness to them, with their gardens and plants."

"That's what we've been told. I'll need to look around myself. Head on back out. You'll need to meet with your staff."

Jake walked away, troubled. He just didn't know what to say to his staff, that one of them was missing, and that there was no idea just why.

Chapter 3

Chani stared out of the window, her concentration on the buildings and parks that they were passing. They were heading to the wrong side of town, to the part that was broken as she thought of it. She didn't like the feeling that she was getting, not at all. She didn't think God would let anything happen to her. Chani then sighed. But that wasn't life, was it, after all? Her parents and her aunt and uncle had been killed, murdered as they had just recently determined. And her cousin, Brinn, had been through something, an adventure as they called it. Only Chani didn't think it was that much of an adventure, not being kidnapped and threatened. But still, she did meet her now husband, Gareth, during the course of that. Chani had prayed for her life mate for years, continuing what her parents had taught her even at an early age. *This is not working,* she thought. *Not at all. I don't want this, Lord. Can't You just release us and let us go our separate ways?*

Ronan watched Chani for a moment, his own heart raised in prayer. His eyes shifted between the windows, Chani, and the three men in the vehicle with them. He too grew concerned as he saw where they were headed. This part of town? It was known for crime. Why had they been taken? That he didn't understand. He was a farmer, not into crime. His friend, Jake? His business was bringing happiness and health to his clients who needed it. That happened through the plants and gardens his staff was responsible for.

—

"Where are we heading? If you're not telling me, I'm out of here." Chani's voice broke through the silence in the vehicle. "Not talking? You need to."

"Just shut up." The man sitting in the front passenger seat snapped at Chani, without turning around. "You're not going anywhere. Not for a long while. If ever."

Chani drew in a deep breath. This was not what she had expected to hear. She would be ready to run as soon as she could. She didn't know Jake and didn't know if he would do the same. She prayed that he would. If not, she was running and that on her own. She knew this part of town only too well. She had searched it many times when they had been looking for Brinn. Chani had developed friendships with some of the people, and she could only pray that they would help her.

Ronan reached once more for her hand, his tight on hers, trying to calm her. Only he didn't think it was working. She was angry, he could tell. He was just afraid that anger would harm her.

The couple watched as the car slowed in front of a building and then headed around behind it. It was well maintained for the area. Chani frowned, not recognizing it. There wasn't a name on it, unusual for buildings in their town.

Ronan waited for the doors of the vehicle to open, surprised when they didn't. He felt Chani's hand tightening on his.

"Well? What are we waiting for?" Chani leaned forward to look around Ronan to glare at the man.

"We're here. Aren't you getting out?" Her fingers had hit the release on her seat belt and on Ronan's. She watched the men carefully, her hand gripping Ronan's tightly.

The two men in the passengers' seats left the car, the driver watching them. Chani's head was moving, before her door was flying open and she was springing from the seat, dragging Ronan with her. Her feet flew across the rough pavement, heading for the building just adjacent to that one and around it, finding a door to open and close behind them. She hesitated before shoving him towards a back wall and done behind a pile of debris.

Ronan crouched beside her, an arm around her and the other one covering their heads. He could hear the sound of pounding footsteps and then the door flying open to bang loudly against the outside wall. Hurried footsteps crossed and re-crossed the floor. Angry accusations flew among the three men.

Chani's breath caught in her throat as she listened. *No,* she thought, *they aren't saying why we were taken. And that I don't get. Lord, this would be a good time for a miracle, don't You think?*

A cross voice interrupted the men and had them spinning to look around.

"Cain't ya be quiet? I'm tryin' to sleep." A man dressed in ragged clothing raised up from what had seemed to be just a pile of debris.

"Where are they?" The first man stood over him, a gun pointed at him.

—

"Ain't no one here but me. And now you. Get out. This is my spot. You're trespassin'.'"

The man's finger tightened on the trigger and then eased off. He tucked the gun away, turning and walking towards his companions.

"Come on. They must have gone right through the building. We'll never find them."

"Yeah, and the boss is not going to be real happy." The driver walked away, secretly admiring Chani and her pluck.

Ronan waited, for what seemed hours, but in reality was not that long. Chani shoved at him and then rose, peeking around the debris and then walking towards the man who now stood watching her.

"George? Is that you?" Chani stopped short of him, a happy look in her eyes. "You're okay?"

"I could be asking that of you and your young man." George watched as Ronan stopped right behind Chani, his hands resting on her shoulders. "Now, what do we do with you two? They'll be hanging around out there, watching to see if you were really in here."

"I know, George. I know that. What can we do?" Unconsciously, Chani leaned back on Ronan, finding comfort in his strength.

"We wait until dark. Here, I have some water bottles and some food. I was out early this morning and grabbed some. God told me that I would have company for a meal." George was away, the door at the back blocked to prevent it from being opened. Beside them once more, he pointed towards the front of the building. "Up there. There are some chairs we can use. We'll get you home, Chani. We could do no less for you."

Chapter 4

Early that evening, George shoved the door open and disappeared, a hand held up to keep Chani and Ronan in the building. He was back within moments, beckoning them with him. They crept out of the building, following him as he kept to the shadows.

Ronan kept Chani's hand tight in his, watching for anything that might bring harm to her. Chani, for her part, was disturbed at that. She kept tugging at it to release it. Only Ronan never let go.

"Chani? Here. Trim will get you to your cars. They're at your work?" George pointed to a ramshackle car.

Ronan stared at the car, not sure that he even want to sit in it, let alone believe that it could and would run. He shut the door after Chani and then slid in behind her.

"Trim? I need to go to my office. Our vehicles are there." Chani chewed at her lip, uncertain for once.

"I know. I'll take you there. The police were in and around there today, Chani. They are looking for you. Where are your phones?"

"In the kitchen, I think, at work. I need to go in and get them." Chani ducked her head as she searched around the car, seeing the reverse trek that they were taking.

Trim pulled up to the building, watching as Chani thanked him and then ran for the building,

—

22

entering and then exiting quickly. Her backpack was in place and their phones were in her hands.

"Here you go, Ronan. Trim, thank you."

Ronan paced beside Chani as she walked to her car. He could see her shooting glances around her.

"Chani? I'll follow you home." His hand went up as she protested. "There is no discussion on this. They know where you work. They may know where you live. Do you have a security system?"

Chani glared at him before she gave an abrupt nod. Once in her vehicle, she drove off, Ronan's truck behind her. She parked in her spot, locking her car after her before heading for the apartment. She sighed. Of course, Ronan would be there, now wouldn't he? She sighed. Her attitude needed work, she knew, and she and God would be having a long talk that night.

Ronan stopped her as she unlocked her door and stepped through, turning off the alarm system.

"Chani? May I walk through for you?" Ronan waited as she stared at him before she nodded. He moved through the apartment and then back to her. "It looks okay. Call me if you need to even if to talk."

Chani sighed, before she nodded. She spun as she heard footsteps.

"Frank? You're here?"

"I am. I had a call that you were on your way home. We need to talk, Chani. Ronan, is it? We need to talk as well. You will tell me what happened today and how you managed to get away. But first, send off

———

a text at least to Eilis or your aunt. They are very worried about you."

Chani nodded, an unreadable look crossing her face.

"I will." Her phone was out and the text sent to her sister. "What happened at the office?"

"Other than you two disappeared, left your vehicles and your phones, and an office was tossed? Nothing." Frank walked through to the kitchen, his briefcase on the table. He reached to flick on the coffee pot, knowing that Chani would have set it ready to go. "Go and change, Chani. I know that you want to. I'll take that time to speak with Ronan. And we will talk, Chani. You will not get out of it."

Chani tried her best to stare down Frank, seeing the amusement in his eyes as she did so. She turned and walked away to her bedroom, the door closed behind her as she leaned against it. She was puzzled by what happened and just why. Chani was also puzzled by Ronan and how he had tried to protect her. She sighed. She would need to apologize to him.

Frank turned to Ronan.

"Ronan, we know each other from church. Sit. I'll get our coffee in a moment but first, tell me what happened." Frank was in his chair, his laptop out and open, and a pad of paper and pen beside him.

"It was just so strange, Frank. Really strange. I mean, there was no one there other than Chani and she said that was unusual. The office was tossed, but I think that was just done to draw her back there. The men didn't ask for anything or say anything other than telling us to leave the building and then for Chani to be quiet." Ronan shook his head. "She was defiant with them, Frank. That could have gone very poorly for her."

Frank grinned even as he shook his head.

"She doesn't look like that, does she? She is a very sweet, compassionate, loving lady. She's had a rough life losing her parents like she did. Ashlynn has done well with Chani, Eilis, and their two cousins." Frank looked towards the hallway, a thought crossing his mind. "What are you up to these days, Ronan?"

"Other than the farm and church? Not a lot." Ronan's eyes narrowed as he studied Frank. "What are you asking?"

Frank sighed, not quite sure how to phrase what he needed to.

"Chani is very independent. She has not been dating. And I know that you are not. She needs someone in her life right now. Someone who can be around with her as she is out and about. Chani won't agree unless it comes from you. If I need to, I can make it a police order. But I would rather not."

"In other words, you want Chani to agree to a boyfriend?" Ronan rubbed his hands down his face. He felt grubby and tired and even to some extent angry. "I can't do that, Frank. I can't just do that." He shoved his statement across the table and then rose, walking away. The door closed quietly behind him.

—

Chani had stopped in the hallway, watching as Ronan had done that. She felt suddenly bereft, needing Ronan to stay in her life. Only she knew that he would walk away from her, just like he had done that night.

"Frank? What happened?" Chani stirred at her mug of tea, watching Frank closely.

"Let's get your statement, Chani. Then, we need to have a serious talk." Frank sighed to himself. This was not going to go well, he thought. Or just maybe it will. He caught the look on Chani's face as she shot glances towards the hallway and the entrance door. There's something going on there, Lord, and it would be nice if these two did stay together for now.

Chapter 5

Chani sat back at last, a frown on her face as she watched Frank. He was up to something she just knew. And that involved her. Her head turned for a moment to look towards where Ronan had walked away. Did it involve Ronan as well? She hoped it did but it not likely did.

"Frank? Now what?'' Chani wrapped her hands around her mug, suddenly deeply afraid.

"Now what? I don't know, Chani, to be honest with you. We need to keep you safe." Frank's look was grim as he tidied away his paperwork and locked it into his briefcase. "We will revisit your adventure with both of you. And not just once. They wanted something from you, Chani, and we need to figure that out."

"I know, Frank. I just don't know what it is. And that scares me. How do I protect myself?"

"You need a boyfriend, Chani. Or at least a male friend who will stick with you when you are out and about." His hand up, Frank waited for Chani to clamp her lips closed. "It's dangerous for you, Chani. You know what you went through with Brinn. I don't want to see your aunt, sister, and cousins go through the same with you. It was enough that you were missing for just one day."

"I don't need anyone with me. I will be just fine." Chani grew obstinate.

Frank rose at last, his briefcase in his hand. He turned at the door, his finger stabbing towards Chani. He was afraid for his young friend, suddenly and deeply afraid.

"I mean it, Chani. Find someone to be with you. If you don't, your aunt and I will." He walked away at her protest.

Chani locked the door, set the alarm, and then paced her apartment. She was afraid, she had to admit. Today had rattled her far too much. The chiming of a text message on her phone had her jumping. Which one of the ladies in her life would that be?

She reached for it, swiping to unlock it and then pull up the message. Her face softened. It wasn't one of her family. Instead, it was Ronan, just checking in he said. Could he interest her in lunch tomorrow? Somewhere they could talk about today? Her fingers flew as she sent a response before she checked her other messages. A group text went to her family and then she headed for bed. Her dreams were not troubled that night, she discovered in the morning. Instead, they were filled with some tall handsome gentleman who promised that he would never let her down and would not let her face whatever it was on her own.

Ronan turned from staring out of the apartment living room window the next morning, a grin on his face as Chani walked towards him. He hadn't really expected her to agree to spend time with him. But there was something that drew her to him, well other than their shared adventure. And they did need to speak about that, he knew. Only he wasn't sure that she would.

———

"All set?" At her nod, he shut the door behind them, waiting as she locked it before he walked her to his truck and then shut the door after her. He paused, feeling someone watching him. Looking around, he could see no one.

"Ronan?" Chani had lowered her window, watching him. "Is something wrong?"

"I'm not sure." He grinned at her before walking around to slide behind the wheel. "Where would you like to go?"

Chani shrugged, not usually in that position. She normally only ate out with her family. She had actually never had a date, she thought. *Now, Ronan walks in and this? We're going out for lunch. God, I'm not sure I am ready to do this. But You seem to think I am. I can't do this on my own, You know. You need to lead here.*

"I don't know, Ronan. I don't know what you like to do or where you like to eat." Chani shifted on her seat, to stare out the window past him. "We need to talk about yesterday."

"We do and we will. But for now, I'm off for a meal with a very beautiful lady. Sad thoughts aren't allowed." He just grinned as her mouth dropped open.

An hour later, Chani sat back in her chair in the restaurant. Ronan had brought her to another town, to a small Italian restaurant. She had not expected that. But she had to admit that it had been nice, to be treated as someone who was precious. She did not remember another man doing that for her since her own father.

Ronan grinned at her, even while shuddering inside. Whoever it was who had been watching him at Chani's had followed them here. He didn't want that to overshadow their day but it would affect it.

"Ronan? What now? Don't you have work to do on your farm?" Chani wasn't sure what all he did.

"No, not really. I just have to check the cattle to make sure that they're okay. That's all. The crops are all in for the winter."

"Okay. So, now what?" Chani rose from the table, taking the hand that he had reached out for her. This was not her, to hold a man's hand, but Ronan was different. He had made her feel cherished and loved over the day. And part of that was making sure that she felt safe.

"I have no idea. There's a river here that we can walk beside. Do you have to meet your family tonight?"

"No, I don't. Not tonight. Tomorrow, we'll get together for lunch. You can come." She grinned at the look of surprise on his face. "I know Frank talked to you. It's what he would do. I didn't hear him."

Ronan sighed, recognizing the elephant in the room and needing to address it.

"He did. He suggest that you needed a boyfriend. I told him that I wouldn't do it just because he suggested it."

"But you want to?" Chani was not shy about asking.

—

30

"As a matter of fact, I do. I would like to explore our friendship. And we have a connection now because of yesterday. And we have still not talked about that."

"No, we haven't. And we need to." Chani sighed. "Can we leave it for the weekend? I know you've been uneasy. So have I. They're going to be tracking us, that's a given. I don't want them to ruin our day."

"And we won't let it. Frank called me early this morning. He does want to talk to us again. I put him off until Monday."

"Monday. Right. That day after tomorrow. The first day of the work week. I guess I have to go to work. I can't avoid that. But I'm not in the office on Mondays. I'm out and about the town with my clients."

"And I can't be with you. I'm tied up on the farm." Ronan stared down at her. He was tall for a man, well over six foot. Yet, he didn't feel that he dwarfed her. Chani's head reached his shoulder, just the right height for him, he thought.

"Then, we'll meet on Monday. Did he say where?" Chani wanted to see Ronan's farm but would not ask. She wanted him to ask her there.

"My place. Listen, I'll pick you up and take you out there. I can grill something for a meal, if you like."

Chani stared at him before she blinked.

—

"Typical male. Always thinking of his stomach." She smirked at him as he stared at her and then began to laugh.

Chapter 6

Ashlynn watched Chani closely the next afternoon, a frown on her face for a moment. She had not been aware that Chani had started to date. Yet here she was with Ronan. Eilis stopped beside her aunt.

"Aunt Ash? Did you know?" Eilis pointed to Chani.

"No, I didn't. I understand that Ronan is the one who disappeared with her on Friday. Maybe they have decided to work together to find out who it was, just like Brinn and Gareth."

"They may have. It's just strange that she didn't say anything last night when we talked."

"She has her reasons. We don't pry, not that you would. We wait for her to tell us."

"And she will at some point, I know." Eilis sighed and walked away to sit near her sister. She caught Ronan watching her and then his eyes moving to the other three ladies and Gareth before coming back to Chani.

"Chani, what happened on Friday?" Eilis dropped to the floor beside her sister. "You've not said."

"We really don't know. We were in the building and then were taken out of it. It was just so strange." Chani was reluctant to talk about it, not sure herself what had gone on or who it had been.

"Do you know who it was?" Darbi spoke up at that point.

"No, we don't. At least, I don't think we do." Chani turned to Ronan. "Did you know them? I thought that you said you didn't."

"No, I didn't, Chani. It was just so strange how it all happened." Ronan was on his feet, heading for Ashlynn to take the tray from her that she was carrying. He served the ladies and Gareth and then sat back down beside Chani, finding her shifting towards him without realizing that was what she had done.

"That's what I don't get." Ashlynn spoke up, her heart sore for her niece. "They didn't ask for anything?"

"Not a thing. And we think the office was tossed to get us back there. It's near the back door." Chani shared a look with her aunt, not sure how to proceed. "I don't know, Aunt Ash. I really don't know what to think."

"Frank is the investigator, isn't he?" Brinn asked the question that they knew the answer to.

"He is. And he's baffled." Ronan set his plate to one side, a hand reaching for Chani's. He didn't see the speculative glances sent their way. "We need to figure this out before Chani is hurt."

"Or you." Chani looked up at Ronan, a puzzled look on her face.

Ashlynn wandered her home after the girls as she still called them and the two men had left. She was deeply concerned, she had to admit. All she could do was pray, she knew, and that she had been doing. She turned as she heard her phone, finding it. Garrett, Gareth's father, had sent a text. Did they need his help, he asked? He had hesitated to contact Chani, not sure if they were at a stage where they needed an investigator. Her fingers tapped against her phone, asking him for help and thanking him.

Chani paced her apartment, not willing to head for bed. She had the lights on low, not wanting a lot of light. She was frustrated and angry. And she had to admit to herself, she was scared. This was unnerving, she decided. And just how did she continue to work and put her clients at risk? She couldn't quit but she would need to have a frank discussion with Jake tomorrow.

Ronan stood in his backyard, his eyes on the stars and moon, communing with his Lord. He too was angry but more than that, he was afraid for the beautiful lady who he now counted as a friend. He wanted to keep her safe. Only he had no idea just how to do that.

The next afternoon, Chani stepped back from the garden that she had been inspecting. The elderly lady approached her, a glass of lemonade in her hand for Chani.

"This is looking so good, Mrs. T." Chani reached to hug her. "It's helping?"

"It is, Chani dear. It really is. Losing my Ralph so quickly didn't give me time to prepare for it. This? This is giving me a reason to get up and get going in the mornings. I love the plants and the colours. You have a rare talent there, young lady, to choose what is appropriate." Mrs. Teeter's husband had died suddenly from a heart attack, leaving her on her own. Jake had approached her one day, asking if she wanted to garden. "Your boss has a wonderful business going."

"That he does. We'll soon be planting the spring bulbs."

"I know. I will miss this. But Jake said that you could help with plants inside. I would like that. I have that sunroom that we can fill." Mrs. T. watched Chani. "Chani, are you okay?"

Chani shrugged, not quite sure what to say. She knew that Mrs. T. went to her church and was a strong Christian. But what had happened to her and Ronan just seemed so personal.

"I guess. It's just everything that went on with Brinn and then finding out that our parents were murdered."

"That would do it. Now, on your way, young lady. You must have someone you're meeting tonight."

"There is, but it's not a date. It's a meeting that I really don't want to go to but I have to." Chani drove away, heading for Ronan's place. She just wasn't sure that was a good idea.

Ronan walked towards Chani, seeing her hesitation. He simply swept her into a hug, a prayer whispered for her in her ear before he dropped a kiss on the top of her head. He had not realized that was

what he had done. It just seemed so natural to do.
Chani felt it in her heart and felt treasured by someone
just for her.

Chapter 7

Frank walked the backyard at Ronan's, gathering his thoughts. He was no closer to knowing who had abducted these two or why. He had spent time with Jake that day, going over clients and their needs and also his suppliers. Jake had a unique business with no competition. But Frank could see where someone would want to take it over. It gave an opportunity for unscrupulous people to move in and take advantage of those whom Jake worked with.

"Frank?" Ronan paced beside him, Chani's hand in his. He had no idea how that happened but it had. He liked that feeling. He wanted to keep this lady safe. Only she was making it difficult for him, wanting to stand on her own feet.

"Ronan? Chani? I'm sorry. We have no idea who it was. We have video feed from around there but they made sure to keep their heads down. And the vehicle was parked in such a way that the license plate was not visible. I'm really sorry. I was hoping to have this solved by now."

"God knows why, Frank." Chani sighed. "I guess I have to tell you what I found on my doorstep this morning." Chani rubbed at her face. Today had not been a good day, not at all. "I found a package. When I opened it, Mom's music box was in it. I thought it was lost. And here it showed up." She blinked to clear her eyes of tears.

"Your mother's music box? What else was in it?" Frank's hand stopped her forward walk.

——

"Nothing. Absolutely nothing. Who does this? Brinn got her father's gloves. Now, me with this. Are they going to this to the others?" Chani was growing angry.

"They may. We'll pray that they don't. I'll need to take a look at that."

"I know. It's in my car trunk. I won't let you have the music box. I don't care about the cardboard box."

"I get that, Chani. Let's get it now and that's done with."

Frank looked the box over, not seeing anything that caught at his attention. It had not been mailed. It simply had Chani's name on the box, in a label that had been computer generated.

"We'll not likely get much from this. I'll take it in." Frank slipped the box into a large bag and labeled it. "Now, the music box?" He gently took it, looked it over and then handed it back. "I don't think that I'll need it. You can tell that it was recently cleaned. And I know you would not have done that."

"No, I wouldn't have. I don't get it, Frank. Who is doing this? You arrested the lawyer when Brinn went through what she did. Who now? And why? Which one of us are they really after?"

"That we don't know. I doubt that this is related to what happened the other day. You both need to take precautions. Ronan, I know that you are here on your own most days. Be very careful." Frank turned to

Chani. "And you, young lady, what are we to do with you?"

Chani shrugged.

"I have no idea. I have to be out and about. You know that. Fridays are the only days that I am in the office. And I don't want this Friday to be a repeat of last week." She paused, a thought crossing her mind. "They have to know my schedule. In order to appear in the office, they had to know that I was there. And how did they know that Ronan was there? Unless he was just incidental to it all."

"That may well be. But now that you two have been out and about together, they will be watching him even closer. You can guarantee that they will go after him to get to you." Frank walked away on those words.

Chani watched him go, not sure if she should be leaving or not. Ronan simply reached to wrap her in a hug, surprising her before she returned it.

"What are we to do with you?" He wasn't sure if he was the one to be asking that question. Chani had become important to him and he just needed to know.

Shrugging, Chani leaned back to look up at him. She was not one to allow men to hug her. So allowing this? This was out of her comfort zone. Or was it? Ronan made her feel safe. Right now, that was what she needed.

"I need to go too, Ronan." Chani reluctantly stepped backwards. "What are we to do about this?"

"I want to talk to Jake and see if he knows what is going on. And Brinn's Gareth has reached out to me. His father wants to speak with us."

"Yes, Garrett will want that. When?"

"He asked if we could meet tomorrow night. Just us." Ronan turned h towards car. "I said that I would speak with you. Drive safely. If you want to stay on speaker phone with me until you get home, we can do that."

Chani stared at him before she slipped into her car.

"So, who raised you?"

She drove away, leaving Ronan laughing at her. His phone rang and he answered it, hearing her laughing voice on it.

"My parents, in case you are interested. They've been away on vacation. But they will want to meet you. That much I know." Ronan turned to walk back towards his home, not looking around. He didn't see the dark form standing near his home, that person's attention focused totally on him.

"Introducing me to the parents? Did we just go somewhere, Ronan, that I didn't know about?"

Ronan's steps slowed as he turned in a circle. He could feel the eyes on him. He just couldn't see anyone.

"I guess we did, Chani. I value you as a friend. If there is to be something more? Only God knows that." He heard the apartment door close behind. "Good night, sweetheart. Sweet dreams." He pocketed his phone, pausing at the bottom of the steps to the back porch before he walked up them and into his house. Yes, he thought, Chani is a beautiful compassionate lady. It shows in her work.

—

Chapter 8

Eilis turned from her sister's doorway, worried about her. She was to meet with her that Wednesday night before they headed off to their ladies' Bible study. There had been no answer. Her car was in her spot. Sighing, Eilis turned back, reaching to unlock the door and head through the apartment, setting down the bag of food that she held.

"Chani? Are you here?" Eilis stood in her sister's bedroom, seeing the clothes on the bed. This was unusual for Chani. She was neat and always put everything away.

Hearing the door open and close, Eilis peeked back out and then walked towards Chani.

"Chani?"

Chani jumped, a small scream coming from her. She stared at her sister, her hand on her chest.

"Eilis? Where did you come from?" Chani's eyes were huge.

"We were to have supper together, Chani. It's on the table. Where were you?" Eilis moved past her sister, not quite sure what was happening but knowing that something was.

"I had to run down to the office for a moment. I'm sorry. I thought that I would be back when you got here." Chani sighed. "This is not going well. I want my life back."

"And why don't you have your life?" Eilis asked the obvious question once the blessing had been said on their food.

"I don't know." Chani chewed her mouthful of food and then swallowed. "Ronan and I met with Garrett last night. He's working on what happened. But it is just so bizarre."

"And it disturbs you and makes you angry." Eilis grinned at her sister. "And you will be out there looking for this person."

"I will. Frank warned me not to. But it is my life, Eilis. Wouldn't you?"

"I would. So will Brinn and Darbi. Aunt Ash as well. Gareth will try and calm you down and stop you from putting yourself out there." Eilis grinned as Chani laughed. She had pegged Gareth so correctly.

"And he will at that. Ronan wants to meet with us all again, just to bounce stuff off of us."

"And just who is Ronan? I mean, we've met him. But I don't really understand how he got involved." Eilis rose to clear away their dinner garbage, an eye on the clock.

"He just happened to be there that day. I am not sure why Jake had asked him. Jake does this sometimes. He asks people to come in for meetings, just for information or for something different or for help on something that he is planning."

"Oh, I get it now. He's planning on having you work on a farm." Eilis continued to grin before she

—

sobered. "Chani? Can we skip the study tonight and just spend time in prayer? I think that we need this."

"We do and we can."

Chani shut and locked the door after her sister. She wiped at a tear, angry with herself for crying. This was not her, she thought. She just needed her mom and dad, and they weren't there. *Who killed them, Lord? And why? Why take parents from little girls who needed them so much? I don't understand that. And I certainly don't understand this, whatever this is, that I'm going so. It would be so nice if it ended tonight. Somehow, though, I don't think it will.*

Ronan stood outside his friend's house. Jake had asked to meet with him again. He hadn't said why, but there had been an urgency to his request.

"Ronan? Thanks for coming." Jake pointed towards his office. "In there. I have coffee there for us."

Sitting into a chair, Ronan studied his friend. Something was going on with him. He just couldn't read him.

"Ronan, I am so sorry that you were taken from my office." Jake's hand went up. "I know. I know. I have apologized already. But it still bothers me."

"Do you know why?" Ronan leaned forward, his elbows planted on the chair arms.

"No. I don't. I wish that I did. Nothing was taken or damaged. That's what is so bizarre. And I don't get why Chani."

—

"Did she see something on one of her jobs that she shouldn't have?" Ronan had been puzzling it out himself.

"That we don't know. We've talked. She's going back over every job that she has been on. But we're not seeing anything."

"For them to come in like that, they have had to be watching us closely. I worry about Chani out on her own."

"And she will not let anyone go with her. I spoke with the detective again today. He has no leads, he stated."

"No, I don't think there is. He did say there weren't any fingerprints or anything like that." Jake was frustrated, to say the least. His friend and his employee were threatened and he had no idea why. "Ronan? How did they know that you would be there?"

Ronan paused as he raised his mug to drink from.

"Are you saying that it's my fault? I have no enemies. At least, not that I am aware of. I thought it had to do with your work." Ronan rose and paced, stopping to lean against the credenza in front of a window. "How do we do this, Jake? How do we determine who took us?"

"That we will do. We need to meet with Chani again. And I am not sure that she will be willing to do that. She told me off this morning for questioning her again." Jake grinned at Ronan's laugh. "She is feisty, Ronan. Just who you need in your life." He smirked at Ronan stared at him, Ronan's mouth dropping open at that.

Chapter 9

Walking through the office building that Friday morning, Chani was uneasy. It had been two weeks since she and Ronan had been taken from it. She didn't feel safe there any more, and she didn't know why. That still angered her. That anger she knew she had to release but wasn't quite ready to do that. Hearing footsteps near her, Chani spun, her hand over her mouth to cover her scream.

Jake watched her, concern on his face. She was not usually this jumpy, he knew.

"Chani? Are you okay?"

"No, I'm not. I don't know that I will be again. Did you really think that I would be?" Chani glared at him, not backing away from his grin. "Sure, you can laugh about it. It wasn't you."

Jake shook his finger at her.

"No, it wasn't me. But it was here in my business. What are your thoughts?"

"My thoughts? That someone made a mistake. That they were after someone else." Chani stomped away, heading for that back office. She stood, feeling something off in there. "Jake? What's different about in here?"

"What do you mean?" Jake stopped beside her, looking into the room and turning his head to study it.

"There's something off in here. Only I don't know what." Chani was into the room, searching

---

before her hand stopped. "This! Where did it come from? It doesn't belong here."

Jake studied the package sitting on the table and sighed. This is getting old very fast, he decided. His hand out to stop Chani from touching the box, he turned her and almost shoved her from the room, closing the door to it.

"Jake! We need to look at it!" Chani's anger flared at him.

"No, we don't. We don't touch it. We leave that for Frank and whoever it is that he brings in. To your office! Now!" Jake's words lashed at her as he became more frightened for his friend and employee.

Chani glared at him once more before she turned, heading for her office. She slumped into her chair for a moment before she tucked away her backpack and then pulled up her schedule for the next week. Fall was in full swing, she decided, and that meant she needed to help her clients clear out their gardens and then plant for spring. She usually enjoyed this time of year but not this year.

Frank paused in the doorway to the office, staring around himself before he walked to the table. The crime scene tech was already there, doing what they did best, he decided.

"What do we have?"

The tech looked around, shaking his head.

"This is strange, Frank. Really strange."

Frank stood, shock on his face for a moment.

—

"You are correct. Dead bulbs. Weeds. Sticks. Pebbles." He looked behind him for a moment. "It really is bizarre. Send me your pictures and any information that you have." Frank's phone was out as he took some photos. "I'll talk to Jake. We need to search, Peggy. We need to see how whoever it was got in. Jake does have a security system."

"I checked. It's off line. Somehow that notification didn't get to Jake. I've a call in to their company to work with them to determine what happened."

Jake stood where he could watch Chani, knowing that she was troubled but also angry and afraid. He had no words for her and had no idea how to help her. He turned his head slightly as he heard Frank stop beside him.

"Frank?"

"Jake? Peggy is reaching out to your security company. The feed was taken down, so we don't have any idea of who left it. We need a list of everyone past and present who has keys."

"I can do that. In fact, I have it already for you. I'll have the locks changed today. Jeff said he would be around in about an hour to do that."

"That works. Also, up your security system. More cameras, strong passwords, etc. You know the drill." Frank turned his attention to Chani, who was watching him. "Chani? What have you gotten mixed up in?"

"I have no idea, Frank. If I did, I would stop it right here and now." Chani was on her feet, moving past them to head for the store room. She stood, her hand holding the door open, anger wafting through her. She was also very scared. Chani just wanted to talk with Ronan, to hear his prayer for her. That puzzled her. She didn't depend on a man, she thought. Why would she want to be with him?

Frank watched her walk away, shaking his head.

"She's running, Frank." Jake gave a quick grin.

"She is. And I am afraid of what she is running towards. There is danger around her, but we don't have enough information to know why. Have you had any calls or letters come in?"

"Not that I am aware of. Jane has not said and she would."

"I did speak with her the other day. I'll speak with her again at some point." Frank walked away, frustrated that this had happened again. He was needed elsewhere but his thoughts were on Chani and Ronan and he did drive away.

Chani heard steps behind her. Jake had walked towards her and stopped, a frown on his face.

"Chani?"

Chani turned, not sure what Jake was up to.

"Jake? How do we do this? Am I too much of a danger to my people?"

"Not that we know of, Chani. It seems that it's here in the office that you are. I am arranging for security to be here over the day for now. They have a car that will pass by here hourly when we're not around. That may help."

"That may help, but it won't stop it." Chani reached for a roll of paper. "I feel like this roll of paper, Jake, when it's dropped. I'm in a free fall of emotions and danger. And because we don't know who it is or who is behind it, we can't stop it." She looked up, trouble on her face, tears that she refused to shed shimmering in her eyes.

Chapter 10

Standing in his barn that afternoon, Ronan stared around. Nothing was out of order, not that he could see, but he still felt something off. He felt threatened and didn't know why. He turned to watch the stock truck move away with the young beef cattle that he had sold for slaughter. He had some that would be going to other farms. He was well known for his excellent cattle.

Sighing to himself, Ronan turned to walk towards his home. A shower would be good, he thought, and then wondered how Chani was. It was Friday night, and he just wanted to take her out for a meal. They had been talking more and more over the last week, not just about what they had gone through. They were finding that they enjoyed one another's company, with many things in common. He reached for his phone. Gareth had been in touch, asking if he could meet with them on the morrow. Ronan had agreed and suggested that Gareth reach out to Chani as he didn't know what she had on.

His phone chiming caught his attention as he pulled on clean socks. He reached for it, not sure who the number was. It was an unknown number. Uncertain as to what to do, Ronan let the message go to voice mail. Listening to it, Ronan's face whitened. He was shoving shoes onto his feet, finding his keys, and then running for his truck. He had to find Chani.

Knocking at Chani's door, Ronan left his hand against it as he looked around. He felt the door move and turned back, finding Chani staring at him.

"Chani? You're okay?" Ronan reached to hug her.

Chani stood, a shocked look on her face, before she shoved against him and backed up. Ronan followed her, shutting the door behind him.

"Ronan? Just what is the meaning of this?" Chani glared at him, seeing the slight amusement on his face. "This is not funny, buster."

"No, it's not. I was just so glad to find you were all right. Sorry, but not sorry that I hugged you." Ronan paced, Chani standing with her arms folded across her abdomen. "I got a voice mail that threatened you. It said that you disappeared. I was so afraid."

Chani stared at him.

"Why would they call you? And not call my family? It's usually the family that gets called."

"I know. That's what they usually do." Ronan's phone was out. "I need to call Frank."

"You can't. He left tonight on a week's vacation. I have no idea who has taken over for him." Chani turned and headed for her office. "I have some work to do, Ronan, that I would like to do tonight. Lock the door after yourself."

Ronan stared after her before he followed her.

"I don't think so, Chani. This is serious." Ronan reached to stop her forward walk.

Chani spun, anger sparking from her eyes.

"I know it is, Ronan. I know that it is. Do you think that I don't know that?" She shoved at him, finding him unmoving. "Ronan?"

"Chani, I treasure your friendship. I don't want to see you hurt. Or your family hurt. I've talked to Gareth. I know what they went through when Brinn went missing. I'm trying to prevent that from happening again."

"But you see, Ronan, it's not up to you. It's up to God. If it's His will that I disappear, then it happens. All I can do is to prepare myself as much as I can." She studied his face, seeing something there that caused her to pause. "Ronan?"

Ronan bit at his lip, not sure how to phrase what he wanted to say.

"Chani? I know that we haven't known each other long. I mean, we're part of the young adults at church. We're in a Bible study together. But this? This is different. I would like to date you, but I'm not sure that you're ready for something like that."

Chani stared at him, shocked before she turned and moved away. She stood at her desk, her hands moving around the work that she had wanted to do that night. Only, it seemed that she wouldn't be doing that.

"Chani, what can I do to help tonight? I would like to take you out to dinner, if you would." Ronan's hands clenched and unclenched before he rested them on her shoulders, stopping her movements.

——

55

Chani turned her head, a thoughtful look replacing the angry one.

"Okay. I guess then that we are dating. But only for now, Ronan. Only until we figure this out. Who can we talk to? I mean I know that Frank is the investigator. But he is also a friend. He will do his best. I just wish I could speak with someone else."

Ronan nodded, knowing that she was echoing his thoughts.

"I have a cousin that we can talk to. He lives just over a town or two. He went through some pretty rough stuff with his wife. Tag will look into this for us as will his friends. Let me call him and see if we could meet with him tomorrow." He groaned as his phone chimed. "Excuse me, Chani. Let me see who this is."

Chani tilted his hand to see the phone screen when he gave a soft laugh.

"Tag? Is that your cousin? How did he know?"

"That's Tag. He's a retired officer. He's ready to head this way tomorrow, with his wife. Can we meet with him?"

Shrugging, Chani walked away, leaving Ronan staring after her.

"Late morning, I think. I am meeting my family for breakfast in the morning. You could always meet Gareth for breakfast." She smirked at him as he laughed. "Now, you promised me a meal. Where are we heading?"

"Jeff's, I think. I like his fish and chips."

Chapter 11

Hearing a vehicle park in his driveway the next morning, Ronan peeked out his front door before he was through it and down to the car. His cousin, Taggart Rafferty, was there. Now, he thought, maybe they could find some answers. But he wasn't sure that they would. There just didn't seem to be enough information for that.

"Tag? It's good to see you." Ronan hugged his cousin and then reached to hug Ayron. "Glad you both could make it. Chani will be here shortly. She was out for breakfast with her family."

"She's related to the Brinn that you talked to us about a while ago?" Ayron reached for the door, to close it behind them as they walked into the house.

"She is. A cousin. There are four of them, two sets of sisters. They had thought for years that their parents died in an accident, but they were murdered. Garrett is working on that, he said. I know Frank still is. But we're not getting anywhere with it."

"How old were they?"

"Young. Brinn was twelve, and there's about a year between each of them. Their aunt took them in, but she was just in her early twenties. It was a large responsibility for her, which she gladly undertook."

"That is." Ayron wandered the downstairs of his rambling farmhouse. "I like the changes that you've made in the last few months. It's very restful."

—

"It is. Mom and Dad were after me to make it my own. I finally have." Ronan shared a look with Tag and then moved to the door, hearing a soft tap at it. "Chani? You're here." Hugging her, he then turned her to face the couple. "This is my cousin, Tag, and his wife, Ayron. We talked about them last night."

"We did, briefly. I didn't know that you had any relatives other than your parents."

Tag began to laugh.

"She's got you there, cuz. Hi, Chani. Ronan seems to think that he needs our help."

"If it solves this, then yes." Chani was disgruntled and trying hard to hide it, seeing the grin on Ronan's face, a matching one on Tag's, and sympathy on Ayron's.

"Let's grab some refreshments and find your back deck, Ronan. I love it. It is so peaceful out here in the country. It's not too cold out there yet."

"No, it's not. You ladies head on out. We'll grab what we need and find you."

Ayron linked an arm with Chani's and walked the yard.

"This was starting to be rundown when Ronan took it over. It had been a maternal uncle's who had had an accident and wasn't able to continue due to a spinal injury. Ronan has worked hard in the last couple of years to bring it back to what it was. His uncle still has a part interest in it but leaves the day-to-day running of it to Ronan."

—

"I didn't know that." Chani stared down at the gardens. "He needs help with gardens."

"He does. You are just the person to help with that." Ayron found a seat in a wicker rocker, watching as Chani perched on the edge of a matching love seat. "He's told us what you do for a living. That has us puzzled as to why you would be targeted. With us, it was someone after what I had in land. And Tag was forced to marry me or else I would have died."

Chani stared at her.

"That doesn't happen in real life." At Ayron's nod and grin, Chani slumped back in her seat. "It won't happen to us. No way."

Ayron began to laugh harder.

"That's what we all said. And there have been a number of friends who went through this." Ayron watched as Tag nodded, taking the mug handed her.

"It's true, Chani. I almost died before I agree to marry Ayron. And she is the love of my life." Tag sipped at his coffee, his eyes on his cousin. "Ronan? What can you tell us?"

"Not a lot. You know that we were taken from the building and then were able to escape. Chani found a parcel at her doorstep that contained her mother's music box. And then tells me that there was a package at the office yesterday containing plant stuff."

"That is odd, that last one. It relates to your work, I would think. But the music box? Who had it?"

———

"We don't know. We want to find out but haven't got a clue where to start. The lawyer who was involved has been arrested. Only, he isn't talking."

"No surprise there." Tag sat back, his eyes on the fields in front of him. "I can start looking into it. And I have friends who can. Just let me know who all is involved and what information that you have."

"Thank you, Tag. I was not expecting that. Just a moment until I check with my family. I will not go behind their backs on this. It is too important to us all."

"Not a problem, Chani."

Chani's fingers flew as she sent off a group text. She was not surprised at how quickly they responded. Her aunt just asked how she knew Tag and when she replied that he was Ronan's cousin, she readily agree. It was time, Ashlynn noted, that they did that. They all needed and wanted the answers.

Ronan reached for Chani's hand, bending his head to pray for her. He looked up, finding her watching him closely. There was an unreadable look on her face which caused him to doubt that they would be able to go ahead with the investigation.

"It's time, Tag." Chani didn't look away from Ronan. "We need to find answers. The only thing that we ask is that you provide your information to Frank. He will need it."

"That we can do. Two of my friends work for someone who is very good at this."

"Emma. She became involved to a certain degree with Brinn's adventure. We had more contact with Richard though and his team."

"You did? Have you talked to him about your adventure?" Tag grinned at her as her head snapped around.

"No, we haven't. I'm hoping to avoid that discussion if at all possible."

Chapter 12

A week later, Chani shoved at her door, trying to close it and lock it. But the force that was shoving against it was too great. She stumbled backwards as the door flew open violently. She screamed, the scream cut off abruptly by the hand clapped across her mouth. She struggled to escape, a lucky blow with her hand striking the man in his eyes. He cursed at her as his hands loosened. Chani took advantage of the loosening of his grip and dodged past him, running for the stairs and then the office, knowing that the manager would be there.

The manager, a man by the name of Stan, looked up startled as Chani flew in, the door slamming behind her. He reached to lock it, pointing wordlessly at the office behind him.

"In there, Chani. I'll call the police."

They heard the hammering at the door and the violent shaking of it. Chani clapped her hands over her mouth to still her scream. Stan shook his head even as he heard the sirens approaching. They could hear the loud curses from the man and then his footsteps thundering away. The sounds of a struggle came to them as Chani slumped down into a chair.

A loud knocking at the door had Chani jumping and screaming. Stan grinned at her as he unlocked the door and opened it slightly, just enough to speak with the officer.

"Chani? Stay here for now. They'll go through your place and then speak with you." Stan handed her a bottle of water that he retrieved from the fridge. "Drink this. It will be a while. Can I call anyone for you?"

Chani sighed, knowing that she needed someone with her.

"Aunt Ash, I guess." She groaned. "Ronan was to be here. He'll be so worried."

"Ronan? I can see if he's out there and get him in here for you. After all, you two are dating, aren't you?"

Chani glared at his grin before she sighed.

"That's what he calls it. I call it trying to solve a mystery. And Aunt Ash is out there as well. She was to drop by about this time."

Ashlynn turned as she felt a hand touch her shoulder. Ronan stood there, worry on his face.

"Ashlynn? Where is Chani?"

"I don't know. I was to meet her here this morning. About this time in fact. She did say that you were to be here as well. What happened? Has she disappeared again?"

The officer who had approached simply shook his head.

"Miss Whitman? Ronan? Come with me. Chani is safe with the building manager. I've been asked to bring you to her."

———

63

"What happened?" Ronan's head was moving, watching the activity around them.

"I can't tell you. All I know is that the manager called us."

Ronan watched as a man was shoved into a car. He drew in a deep breath. That was the man who had walked them out of Chani's work. He had been here? She was in more danger than they knew.

Ashlynn wrapped her niece in her arms, a prayer whispering in her ear. She nodded at Stan, a mouthed thank you sent to him. Stan nodded, before he turned to his phone, which was ringing incessantly.

Ronan watched as Chani stepped back from her aunt, her eyes finding his. She was in his arms, clinging to him. Sobs shook her for a moment.

"Chani? That man? He was here?" Ronan's question caught Ashlynn's attention.

"The man? Which man?" Ashlynn was puzzled.

"The man who was there at my work. You know. The one who made us leave with him." Chani was snapping at them, frustrated and afraid.

"Him?" Ronan spun to stare at the door. "How did you get away?"

"I struggled with him. I don't know how I managed to get away, but I did. Stan kept me safe." Chani kept her eyes on Ashlynn, seeing how her aunt was struggling to accept this. "Aunt Ash?"

"How do we do this, Chani? How do we keep you safe? He's come right to your home."

———

"I know, Aunt Ash. I know that. I don't know how we do that."

Stan had been watching her closely, his gaze shifting to Ronan. He nodded. There was interest there, he thought. But neither one is ready for anything further, if they ever will be.

"We'll do what we can, Chani. The rest of the tenants are on board with what we do. We're putting locks on the door and you'll need to unlock the front door to come in. Anyone coming in will have to be let in by you. We understand that this will not be for the long term. But for now, this is what we do to keep you safe. I know that your families have keys to your apartment. We'll make sure that they have keys to the door. Anyone else?"

Ronan spoke up, his eyes on Chani.

"I would like one, Chani, if I may."

Chani stared at him, her eyes narrowing as she tried to stare him down. She caught the grin that he was trying to suppress. He expected her to say no, but Chani was stubborn enough to prove him wrong.

"That works, Stan. He's around enough as it is. He may as well have a key to that door." She shuddered for a moment. She could feel the danger coming closer to her and her loved ones. That she didn't know if she could handle. She did not want to see anyone of her family or friends hurt. And that was exactly what she was afraid would happen.

Chapter 13

Ronan stared around his barn. Something was off, he decided, and began his search. He sighed. Yes, he thought, they have been here and placed cameras around here. They won't catch anything but the cattle. This was just so bizarre, he thought. Chani doesn't come out here, if she was the one that they were after. He paled as a thought crossed his mind. Reaching for his phone, Ronan called Frank, just getting his voice mail.

"Frank. It's Ronan. I'll need you to head my way. There are cameras around my property. And I have a thought. What if Chani is not the one that they were after? What if it was me? And they're trying to take her to get to me, thinking that would work. Call me please."

Frank turned from the crime scene that he had been on, listening to Ronan's voice mail. It was what he had been expecting. What he hadn't been expecting was Ronan's question. He had to admit to himself that thought had crossed his mind. He walked towards his car, calling for the crime scene team to head for Ronan's. This just made his long day already longer.

Frank's eyes turned to the car that he had followed into Ronan's driveway. The man exited and walked towards Ronan, who stood staring at the two vehicles. Law enforcement, Frank thought. He walked towards the two men, finding them turning to study him.

"Frank? I didn't expect to see you."

"I heard your voice mail. I have a team on the way once they've cleared the scene that they are working on. It's been very busy." Frank turned towards the barn. "Where all are they?"

"The barn for sure. The garage. And I think around the house. I just don't get why."

"They need to watch you, Ronan. Just to see if Chani comes around here." Tag shook his head at his cousin. "That's what they do. We had that."

"I know that you did. I was just praying that it wouldn't happen to us. Chani just managed to escape the man yesterday at her home."

"That's what she told Ayron. Ayron sent me this way. I dropped Ayron off with Chani at her work. Jake is okay with that, he said."

"He is. I still don't understand." He turned to find Frank watching them closely. "This is my cousin, Tag Rafferty. Ex-officer. He and his wife, Ayron, went through some pretty hard stuff."

Tag nodded, his eyes searching the area.

"That we did. It was brutal. May I call you Frank?" At Frank's nod, he sighed. "This is not what we wanted to find. Not here. Ronan, what do we do with you?"

Ronan shrugged, not sure himself.

"I just want to keep Chani safe. And I don't know that we can even do that. How do we?"

"It's not going to be totally possible, Ronan. I know that from first-hand experience. We do the best we can."

"I talked with Richard." Frank spoke up at last, running scenarios through his mind. "He is willing to speak with you two and try to come up with ways to do that. Only he doesn't think it is going to be possible either."

"No, it isn't. She is out and about with her work and with her friends and family. There is just no way that we can have someone with her all the time."

"And she won't take that. I know her that well." Ronan turned and walked towards the barn, the two men walking with him. "In here, Frank. I don't know why they would be doing this for. I haven't any enemies."

Frank stood in the entrance to the barn, looking around and then up.

"Your loft?"

"I've been up there. I can see where it has been disturbed. I didn't look around too much, thinking that you would need to do that."

"We will. How be you two head for the house? I'll look around." Frank stepped outside to find the crime scene team walking towards him. "We'll be a while."

Frank walked slowly towards the house late that afternoon. Or was it early evening, he asked himself. He was exhausted and the day was not over yet. Not by a long shot. There were just too many cases in the queue and that distressed all of the investigators.

Ronan sighed, seeing the look of defeat that momentarily showed on Frank's face. *He didn't find anything, now did he, Lord? And we are no further ahead in finding whoever this is or why. I want this over for my lady and her family. I need to find out who and why. Only I'm not sure how to do just that.*

Tag's gaze flickered between Ronan and Frank, before he nodded. This was where his friends would come in. And of course, he had reached out to Emma. Evan, who worked remotely for Emma, was working on it as he could. They all planned to arrive here in the next few days, just to go over everything with the couple. And there was a lot to go over. Her family would need to be involved as would Ronan's.

"Frank? What did you find?" Ronan's voice finally broke through the silence.

Frank looked up from the meal that Ronan had provided for him. He was grateful for that. He had been told to go off the clock. Another investigator had taken over for the weekend. Frank was grateful. He was feeling worn out, burnt out, and discouraged. His prayers for his friends didn't seem to be going anywhere. But he knew that God heard. That was a given, he thought. God knew where this was going. He was also confident that there was someone out there that God was using Ronan and Chani to reach. Frank only wished that they didn't have to face danger.

"A number of cameras. And this." Frank held up his phone, a photo showing. "They have been following both of you, which is what they will do. And this is where it is going to get a lot harder for you both. Richard called and said that he would be meeting with you two in the next day or so. Listen to what he has to say. No one will force you to do what he is suggesting. All we want is for you two to be prepared. He will go over different scenarios with you and give suggestions on what you both can do.”

“Thank you, Frank. I appreciate that. Tag and his friends are working on this as well. They will be here on Saturday.” Ronan sighed once more, his eyes on the fields that were barely showing in the fading daylight. “I am just glad that the field work is done. And most of the beef that I needed to move out are gone. That makes it a lot easier.”

“It does in one way, but it makes it harder in another.” Tag spoke up. “You’ll have more time to worry.” He smirked as Ronan made a face at him.

“I know that. And Chani is just going to keep working. I talked to Jake. She’s about done with the outside work for now and will be working inside with the clients that want that. It makes her work lighter. She spends more time inside at the office or working from home during the winter.”

“That helps but also makes it more difficult to work with her.” Frank stood at last, his eyes on the tabletop before he looked up. “This is difficult for you, Ronan. You can’t smother Chani, no matter how much you want to. You will have to let God protect her. And that is always difficult to do, to take our hands off a situation and step back.”

———

Chapter 14

Chani's footsteps slowed as she walked towards Ronan on Saturday morning. Her cousins and sister were with her. Her aunt had another commitment and wasn't able to come.

"Chani?" Brinn's voice broke into her thoughts. "What are you thinking?"

"I have no idea. I don't know what to think. Not any more. How did you ever get through it, Brinn?"

"God. You all. Aunt Ash. And of course, Gareth. His family."

"And we'll get you through this as well." Darbi's gaze shifted between her cousin and Ronan. "Ronan's watching you closely, you know."

"I know that he is. I am just afraid that he is going to get hurt really bad." Chani stuffed her hands into her jacket pockets. "And I know that I can't live with myself if that happens."

"He won't look at it that way." Eilis turned as she heard other vehicles. "Who all is here?"

"His cousin, Tag and his wife. And other friends who have agreed to help us." Chani walked into Ronan's hug, feeling his arms tighten around her. She felt safe and treasured. "Ronan? What am I to do with you?"

"Love me." His voice was low enough that only Chani could hear him. He raised his voice. "Now, that we are all here, tell us about these lamp ornaments that you all have. I've seen yours, Chani. Gareth mentioned yours, Brinn."

"Our lamps." Chani leaned back enough to look up at him, seeing the look in his eyes that she had always dreamed of seeing in a man's eyes when he looked at her. "Aunt Ashlynn always told us about the five wise virgins in the parable in the Bible. She told us that we were to have our lamps bright and shiny, ready to be that witness for God that we needed to be. That we needed to be ready to live for him. But also that if He asked us to die for Him, then we needed to be ready to do that too."

"I like that thought. You do that, you know." Ronan turned her to face his friends and introduced her. "Now, let's see what we can accomplish today. I know these guys have been working hard on this, as much as they can."

Two hours later, Chani rose, her eye on the clock. She walked towards Ronan's kitchen, finding Eilis there, staring into the fridge.

"Is there something in there that will bite you?" Chani grinned at her sister. "He said he has food."

"He does. What did he do, buy out the store?" Eilis reached for the sandwich that Ronan had prepared, the trays of veggies, and turned to set it out. "Do you know where his plates and that are?"

"Here. He said we would use disposable stuff, as he called it today. That way, none of us will have to be tied up to cleaning up." Chani didn't see the looks that Eilis was shooting her away. She turned as she heard footsteps and Ronan appeared in the doorway.

—

"Oh, good. You found the food. We'll just set it out here and then everyone can help themselves." Ronan simply reached to wrap Chani in a hug, seeing her distress. "We're making progress, sweetheart. We are. We'll take a break and then go back at it."

Eilis eyed them before nodding. Chani had found her fellow, just like Brinn had. Did it take them being in danger before they did?

"One thing I don't understand, Chani. Where was that music box? And what else is missing that we don't know about or have forgotten about?"

Tag spoke from behind Ronan.

"That's a question that we were tossing around just now, Eilis. As Ronan said, we'll eat and then spend time in prayer. It's what we do."

Two hours later, the group was back at work, papers passing between them. There was quiet conversation and the occasional burst of laughter as they teased one another.

Chani sat and watched them, a puzzled look on her face. She stared down at her paperwork before she rose, to head for the outdoors and pace. Ronan had watched her and then risen to follow her.

"Chani? What did you discover?" Ronan paced beside her.

"I am not sure." She turned to look towards the house. "I know that the lawyer has been arrested. But there has to be someone else out there. There are two sets of people, aren't there?"

—

"That's the conclusion we have come to. One after you. One after your family. Only we don't know why there are two."

"We have determined that. I just don't know why." Chani began to pace again, her arms wrapped around herself.

"I don't know either. I wish I could solve this today. I fear it is only going to get worse." Ronan stood watching her, his hands clenching and unclenching.

"I know it is. I just wish.." Her voice died away as she turned once more, heading for the house, leaving Ronan standing there, his head dropping in frustration.

"Ronan?" Evan, a friend of Tag's, stood nearby. "What can we do for you two? I mean, we are working on this. Emma has told me to concentrate on it and she'll work on it as she can. And we are praying for you. But there has to be something that we can do."

"I would like to take her away for a day, just to get away from the stress. Only, I don't think that's such a good idea. Whoever it is will go after her family to get to her."

"I know. They can do that." Evan shared a look with Shea, who had also approached. "We can get you to our place for a day. We're not really that far apart. We can car pool if you like."

Ronan nodded, his eyes on the field behind the house. He suddenly was running that way, startling the two men with him. They exchanged a look and then were running after him, not sure what was going on but knowing that Ronan would not have reacted like this without a reason.

Chapter 15

Ronan slid to a stop, his eyes on the man standing there. He didn't know him. He sensed Evan and Shea flanking him.

"Who are you? You are trespassing?" Ronan waited for the man to respond. When he didn't, he reached for his phone.

The man's hand went up.

"Wait, Ronan. Don't call anyone yet. I couldn't come to your house. I need to keep our contact as quiet as I can."

"But who are you?" Ronan reached out for the business card handed to him. He looked down and then back up in surprise. His mouth opened as he started to speak, snapping it closed as the man shook his head. "You don't want to be named out loud?"

"Not at this point. I just wanted to warn you and your lady. There is more at play here than what you have come up with likely or what you could expect. Here. Take this. I know your friends will look into it. Before you hand it over to Frank, work through it." He turned and walked away, disappearing before some trees.

Ronan stared after him, a puzzled look on his face. *Who was he, Lord? And what did he really want? I am confused here.*

"Ronan? Do you know him?" Evan's quiet question caught at Ronan's thoughts and brought his face around to Evan.

"No, I don't know that I do. But he does look familiar. I wonder why."

Shea nodded. He had recognized the man, an undercover officer who he had worked with previously.

"He's undercover, Ronan. I know him and trust what he has brought to you. Only don't ask me for his name. I won't give it."

Ronan stared at Shea before nodding. He had that figured out. Only what had he been given? He fingered the envelope, not sure that he wanted to open it.

"Let's see it, Ronan." Evan reached for it, his eyes on Ronan.

"I just don't get it, Evan, Shea. Why me? What did I do?"

"Nothing, except become a friend to Chani, I would suspect." Shea leaned closed to look at the material. "This is helpful, Ronan. He's listing names, addresses, and connections. Let's head back to your house and make copies for us all. Do you have a safe that you can lock this away in?"

Ronan nodded, his eyes on his friends. Tag had appeared at last, his hand reaching for the material.

"Ronan? What is this?"

Ronan shrugged.

"Some guy appeared, handed me that, and then walked away. It's bizarre." Ronan walked away from them, suddenly desperate to find Chani and ensure that she was okay.

"He's worried, guys." Tag watched his cousin. "And for once, I don't know what to say to him to help."

"There's not much we can say. We know how it was with all of us. All we can do is support him and Chani and try to solve this." Evan walked after Ronan, catching up with the other man as he had stopped to stare down at the envelope. "Ronan?"

"What is this, Evan? I mean, it's material, but will it help at all?"

"That's what we'll need to determine." Evan's hand on his shoulder directed him towards the house where Chani stood, watching him.

"Ronan?" Chani's quiet voice brought his head up and he simply wrapped her into his arm. "What do you have there?"

"An envelope supposedly with information that we need." He turned her towards the house. "Let's go in, make our copies of it, and then work on it for a while. We're not working a lot longer before we quit for the day. We need that break, sweetheart."

Chani looked up at him as he called her "sweetheart". He had been doing that all day. She just didn't understand why. She would need to ask him that. Some day, she thought.

—

The others looked up as Ronan handed out copies of what he had been given. They were surprised at what had happened, Tag shaking his head at Ronan. They would talk later, he decided. For now, they would work through what they had.

Chani wandered her apartment late that night. She was exhausted, feeling very overwhelmed but also uncertain at the amount of material that she had been bombarded with that day. Just where it would lead she had no idea. Ronan had called her not that long before, just to say good night and to make sure that she was okay.

Ashlynn had dropped in around an hour earlier, just to hug her niece and pray with her. She was concerned about her, not sure how to express what she needed to say. Chani had simply looked at her and then hugged her once more, sending her on her way. At the moment, all Ashlynn could do for her was pray for her. That was not a problem, she knew. She had been praying for Chani and the other girls since they were born and more so now that they were facing whatever it was. She was certain that it would not end with Chani and that thought made her fearful.

Turning the lights out at last, Chani curled up in her favourite armchair, her eyes on the night sky. She had opened the drapes and then the sheers, needing to watch the sky. The twinkling of the stars always humbled her. Just why that was, she could never explain when asked. The only thing she could say was that God loved her and set the stars as lights to remind her of that love.

—

Chapter 16

Ronan watched as Chani walked towards him two nights later. She had called him, asking if they could meet to talk. He had readily agreed, asking her to go out for a meal. He had parked in her apartment building lot, finding her waiting for him. She was agitated, that much he could tell. Ronan knew that he would eventually find out.

"Chani?" He simply swept her into a hug, finding shudders shaking her body. "What happened?"

Chani shrugged as she stepped backwards, not wanting to look at him.

"Where are we eating?"

"At Jeff's. It shouldn't be that busy right now." He tucked her away in his truck and then stood for a moment, his eyes on her as she shifted uncomfortably on the seat. Something had happened since they had been in church yesterday, that much he could tell. Now he had to get her to tell him. And he wasn't sure that he could even do that.

Chani shoved her plate aside, her eyes on Ronan. She could feel other eyes watching her, some kindly, but there was one set that she could feel the hatred from. Only she didn't know which person that was and if they were male or female. Ronan simply reached for her hands, bowing his head to pray for her.

"Chani? What happened? I know something has."

Nodding, Chani struggled to find the words to express how she felt. This was not easy, she knew. A friend of Ronan's had approached her, and she had had to turn and run from him. There had been such a presence of evil surrounding the man.

"How close of a friend are you with Jeremy Black?"

Ronan was taken aback by her question, not sure where that had come from.

"Jeremy? Not that close. Not really. We were through school together. I see him the odd time around town, but I can't say that I've spoken with him in years. I avoid him. Why?"

"He approached me today as I was leaving one of my job sites. He has to have been following me. He warned me about you, said that you were evil, and that I should not even speak with you. He was gone before I could say anything in response. I ran for my car and headed home. Then you called."

"Jeremy did that?" Ronan sat back, thinking through her words before nodding. "Yes, that would be him. He's trying to break us up, I suspect. Did you know him before?"

Chani shook her head.

"No. I had seen him around with an acquaintance. But I have never ever spoken to him. I don't get why he would do or say what he did. I called Frank but had to leave a voice mail." Chani blew out a breath. "I don't like this, Ronan. There are just too many threads to this."

—

"There are. We need to pull at a few to try and figure out what's going on." Ronan studied her, hating that the lady who was claiming his heart was in distress. "I'm sorry, Chani. That should not have happened. Let's walk, shall we?"

Her hand tight in Ronan's, Chani walked through the downtown area, smiling at acquaintances and friends. Ronan studied her as best he could in the dimming light. He sighed to himself. This is not what he had wanted that night. He had just wanted some time with his lady and to try and get her to smile for him. Only, that wasn't working out so well.

"Chani? What is your work like for the rest of the week?"

"I'm in the office for now. I only need to go out to the clients who I have over the winter a couple of days a week. Jake has told me that I can work from home if I need to." Chani bit at her lip. "I might do that. I feel that danger is moving in and that I am putting my work mates at risk."

"They won't see it that way, I doubt. Jake told me that he had talked to them all. All of them are worried about you and you alone. They are not at risk. They don't want to see you stop working in the office."

"I just worry about them." Chani's footsteps slowed as she stopped walking. "Ronan, where do we go from here? Frank called today. He doesn't have enough information to continue the investigation and he has to set it aside for now. He doesn't like to do that."

"No, there isn't enough information. My friends are working on it. Emma will as well but she and Abe are away with his team and she's working through urgent cases right now. Jace will work on it as he can but they have a backlog of information that they are trying to find."

"I appreciate that. We can't move on with our lives while this is still over us." Chani's foot raised to walk forward, the motion stopping as Ronan simply wrapped her into his arms.

"We can go on with our lives, Chani. I would like to date you. You are a beautiful, compassionate lady who I want to keep in my life." Ronan didn't look at her, afraid of what he would see on her face.

"Ronan? Do you mean that?" Chani held her breath as she stared up at him, wondering that she had found someone so tall, like her father had been. She waited almost breathlessly for his response.

Ronan nodded at last, his eyes dropping to her face. The look on it gave him hope that just maybe his feelings were returned.

"I do, Chani. God brought us together, for some reason. I just don't want to let you go." Ronan found himself the recipient of a sudden hard hug before Chani paced away from him, heading back towards his vehicle.

He stood in shock for a moment before he ran after her, his hand reaching for hers. They had just gone somewhere in their friendship, he knew, but he also knew that Chani would not back down from whoever it was that was after him. He could tell that

she was growing angry once more. Ronan had to admit
to himself that he was as well.

84

Landing facedown in one of his fields, Ronan struggled to escape the hands holding him down. His struggles were in vain. He didn't speak, couldn't speak as a gag was slapped over his mouth. He finally stopped struggling, listening to the men around him. There were at least two he knew. That was what he figured, he thought.

Hauled to his feet, Ronan was pushed towards the back of the field, away from his farm buildings. Fear grew in his heart. He had no idea who had captured him but someone had. And that someone not likely had the good of his health in mind. He stumbled, barely keeping to his feet, his hands bound behind him.

Shoved roughly into a vehicle, Ronan slumped back against the seat, his eyes turned back towards his property. He then turned to study the man beside him, a frown on his face. He should know the man, he thought. Only he didn't. And he didn't know the two men who were in the front. *God, where are You? Are You here? Please, dear Lord, help me to get away. Protect my lady. Keep her safe. And if I don't get back, please comfort my family, Chani, and my friends.*

Ronan jumped as a blindfold was dropped over his face, darkening his world and leaving him feeling helpless. He struggled to avoid it but couldn't avoid the blindfold. Not a word was spoken. He lost track of time, only knowing that the vehicle had been travelling for a while both in a city and in the country. Ronan wasn't sure if he was still in his home area.

—

The vehicle finally slowed and turned into a driveway. Ronan felt the vehicle shift two of the men got out. He knew the man beside him remained in it. He shifted away from him, trying to determine if he really could get away. Only, he wouldn't be able to. Not with bound as he was.

Ronan was finally hauled from the vehicle, a hand on his arm leading him towards a building. He was shoved inside, barely able to keep to his feet. He staggered for a moment, finding his balance and then standing still. His head twisted as he listened, sighing as he realized that he was on his own. Still bound, he had no option but to stay exactly where he was.

How long he stood there, he was never sure. He could see the day darkening around the edges of his blindfold. He dropped at last to the floor, shuffling himself until he could sit without sitting on his legs. He had no idea where he was. That scared him beyond anything that he had ever experienced. Ronan prayed as he had not prayed before, but he had no confidence that his prayers would allow him to be released.

One of the men stood in the open doorway, his eyes on Ronan. He was angry, he admitted. He had now become involved in something that he had been adamant he would not. *A kidnapping,* he thought. *What have I done? And how do I get out of here?* He simply turned and walked away, the door swinging behind him.

Ronan turned as he heard a noise and shifted to his knees before he made his way to a wall. He used the wall to find his feet, catching an arm on an exposed nail. He paused before he began to rub at the ropes

———

86

binding him. Ronan could feel the rope separating thread by thread. After what seemed like hours, he broke the final thread. He stood for a moment, unable to move his arms. Then he brought his arms to the front of his body, shrugging his shoulders and moving his arms to loosen the stiffness. He began to rub at his wrists, feeling the dampness of the blood on them. Ronan undid the gag and then the blindfold, using the cloths to bind around his wrists.

Stumbling to his feet, he moved around the building, seeking a way out. Ronan paused as he felt the door move under his hand. *Lord, is this for real?* He paused, not wanting to walk out into an ambush. The door swung open but he still hesitated. *Lord, can I leave? Where am I, though? Am I near home?*

Ronan peeked around the door, not seeing anyone in the dusk. He sighed to himself. He didn't know the area and had no idea of where to go to head for safety. *Lord, this is where You need to lead me. Guide my steps, dear Lord, back to my lady and my family. I don't know that I will make it, though. It's dark here. I have no idea where I am.*

Ronan's steps led him to a road, where he hesitated, not sure which way to turn. He finally walked to his right, hoping and praying that he was heading for home. He shrugged deeper into his jeans jacket, knowing that it would not be enough to keep him warm over the night. The temperature was dropping and he could feel the change. He dug his hands into his jeans pockets, hunching his shoulders to try and keep warm. His head tilted back and he stared

—

at the clouds moving in. *This is not good,* he thought. *Those look like rain and I have no shelter.*

Ronan's footsteps halted after a while. He was stumbling as he walked, the cold and fatigue drawing him down into a space that he had no desire to be part of. His head dropped for a moment before he wiped at the drizzle covering his face. He was chilled right through. Ronan's steps picked up once more as he trudged forward, not sure where he was heading but with the confidence that he was heading in a direction to find help.

Ronan's steps stopped once more before he dropped to the ground. He just could not go on, he decided. He peered around in the darkness, seeing nowhere that he could see shelter. *Lord, tell my lady that I love her. Don't let her grieve. And my family? Let them know too how much I love them. Protect them all.*

Ronan slumped even further to the ground, his body lying in a pool of water. He didn't feel it soaking into his clothes and the chill soaking into his body. He just didn't feel anything.

Footsteps approached him as a man came to a stop, his eyes on Ronan. Ronan had not seen the shadowy figure following him since he had walked away from the building where he had been held captive. The man crouched down, a hand on Ronan's shoulder before he stood once more. He searched the area around him before his gaze went to Ronan once more. He reached to pull Ronan to his feet, an arm around the younger man. He helped Ronan to stand and then walk forward.

Their walk took them towards a cabin, hidden from sight, not far from where Ronan had collapsed. The man stood for a moment, watching Ronan, before his hand directed the younger man to a bathroom and a hot shower. Clean and dry clothes were left for him.

Ronan's eyes were blurred from fatigue and the fever that he was now beginning to fight. He coughed, a rough harsh cough. He sighed to himself as he dressed, rubbing at his hair with a dry towel. Gazing around, he frowned. This was not his home. He just didn't know where he was. Opening the door, he walked forward towards the heat that he could feel before his eyes rolled back and he collapsed. The man was at his side, a hand on Ronan's wrist before he lifted Ronan and carried him to a bunk not far from where Ronan collapsed.

"We have a fight on our hands, Lord. A fight to save this young man. The rough treatment that he experienced earlier as well as the soaking is not working in our favour. And I can't leave him to seek for help." The man worked away, using what he had available before he stood back. His eyes searched the cabin, looking for help that wasn't there.

Chapter 18

Chani walked through the downtown area of her town, seeking Ronan and not finding him. Tag had called her early that morning, simply asking if she had heard from him. He had sighed as she had said no.

"Tag? What are you not saying?" Chani had stood at her living room window, staring down at the car that kept circling the parking lot. It was not one that she had seen before.

"He's not here, Chani. It doesn't look as if he was here last night." Tag walked towards the barn, knowing what needed to be done. He had helped his cousin many times. "I'm doing what I can and then I'm starting a search."

"But it rained last night. You won't find anything, now will you? Call Frank, please." Chani stared down at her phone before she tossed it to the couch. She had waited for Ronan's nightly call, a call that never came. Now she knew why.

Reaching for a jacket, Chani tucked her phone and wallet into a pocket. She locked her door behind her and then headed for her vehicle. It was Saturday, and she and Ronan had planned to spend the day with her family. Now, that wouldn't happen. She had simply sent a text message to her sister, asking her to pray and that Ronan seemed to have disappeared. She had ignored the chiming of the text messages that responded.

She could hear footsteps following her, stopping whenever she did. She took a look behind her and nodded. Frank was there and his eyes were not on her. They were on a man who was dogging Chani's path. He looked around, nodding at a plains-clothes officer to move in and arrest the man. Chani turned slightly as she heard a small commotion but then shrugged and went on her way. She knew that if she needed to know something, Frank would be in touch.

Eilis watched her sister walk towards, reaching to hug her.

"Chani? Where's Ronan? Weren't you two to come to lunch with us?" She frowned at the look on Chani's face.

"He's missing, Eilis. Tag was at his place this morning. He's not there and hasn't been since yesterday."

"He's what?" Eilis' voice rose and then fell before she looked around. A hand on Chani's arm drew her sister into a cafe and then to a booth. Eilis watched her closely, not sure what was up with her.

"He's missing." Chani was growing angry. "We need to find him. Only I don't know where he would be. Tag didn't have a lot of information."

"Then, we'll work it. Eat up, Chani. Then, we find our cousins and Aunt Ash and see where we go. Gareth said his father was weighing in on this."

"Garrett is? Okay." Chani dropped money on table to pay for her meal and stalked away, leaving Eilis staring after her.

—

"Chani? Wait up? Where's your car?"

"At home. I walked here and I'm walking home. If you drove, I'll meet you there."

Eilis stared in shock as Chani simply walked away. No, stomped away, Eilis thought. She sighed, heading for her vehicle, stopping as she saw Evan and Shea watching her, an amused look on their face.

"Eilis? Fighting with your sister?" Evan reached to hug her before he turned her in the direction that Chani had walked towards.

"No. She's not being reasonable. She's angry and that scares me."

"Tag called us. Are you heading home or to Chani?"

"To Chani's. We're planning on working on this. I need to call the others."

"They're on their way there. Flannery was speaking with your aunt earlier and mentioned that we were in town. She asked if we could meet at Chani's."

"Okay. Let me get my car and I'll meet you there." Eilis frowned as Shea walked with her. "Shea? You were with Evan, weren't you?"

"I was and right now, I'm with you. They'll go after one of you three to get to Chani. We think that your aunt is safe for now." Shea's face grew grim. "We need to go over some things with you. What to watch for. How to keep yourselves safe."

<hr>

"And just how do we do that, Shea? We don't know who it is that is after Chani. Or is it Ronan that they are after? How valuable is his property?"

Shea nodded. Eilis had asked the very question that Shea had asked Evan that morning.

"It is potentially worth millions. For development. There are rumours of minerals on it. Emma is looking into that but she has other investigations that she has to do on an urgent basis."

Eilis shot Shea a look, shock on her face.

"That much? But it's just a farm."

"It is just a farm, but it is in a very good position for a developer to move in and take it over. And that is just if that person is on the up and up. Illegal activity would be worth much more."

Eilis grew quiet even as she parked beside Chani's car. She sat for a moment, her thoughts muddled.

"I didn't know that. Would Ronan?"

"I would imagine that he does. Now, are you ready to go in or will we just sit here in your car discussing the weather?" Shea grinned at her as she opened her mouth to reply and then snapped it closed.

Chani watched as Eilis walked rapidly towards her, Shea keeping step with her. He was alert, she saw, his head moving as he searched the area. *Yes,* she thought, *we are in danger, and just why is what I would like to know. Lord? How long does this go on? I want it over yesterday. I can't live like this. And Ronan needs to come home.*

Chapter 19

Chani dropped her papers onto the kitchen table before squinting at the clock. They had been working away all morning, Frank appearing at one point. Ashlynn turned to simply hug her niece, not sure what words that she could say that would help.

"Aunt Ash? Where is he?" Chani's voice held a wobble, showing how strong her emotions were at that point.

"He's in God's hands, Chani. Those are not just rhetoric. We believe that. As difficult as it can be, it is the truth. Now, about that letter you are trying to hide from us?" Ashlynn smiled sadly as Chani wiped at her eyes.

"That letter. It was on my door this morning. Someone had to get in the building or else one of my neighbours are involved." Chani didn't hear the quiet sound from Frank as he heard her words.

Frank turned, finding Evan and Tag beside him.

"Did we look at her neighbours?"

Frank nodded.

"We gave them a cursory look, but I'll be looking harder at them. There is no way that they should have been able to get into the building. Not unless someone gave them a key or they managed to pick the lock." Frank walked away, the apartment door closing quietly behind him, as he headed for the manager.

Eilis shared a look with her cousins before Darbi was on her feet and hugging Chani.

"Chani? We need you to start writing everything down. A diary of sorts, if you want to call it that. Going back as far as you can. This just didn't start when you were taken out of the office. This has to have started before that."

"I know, Darbi. I know. I just wish I knew if it was related to me, to Ronan, or back to Mom and Dad. Aunt Ash? Have we heard anything more on that investigation?"

"No, we haven't, and we should have. I'll speak with Frank and see if he can find out anything." Ashlynn looked around at the younger ones scattered through the apartment. "How be we pack this up for the day? Head over to my place and have some food? We need to clear our brains and sitting here and worrying over the papers isn't doing that."

Darbi agreed, reaching for Chani once more to hug her cousin.

"Please, Chani? Can we do that?"

Chani kept her eyes on Tag, a puzzled look on her face. Tag waited, his arm around Ayron, waiting for Chani to refuse. She could see the grin that he was trying hard to hide.

"I think that is a very good idea, Aunt Ash. Let's head that way. I have some squares and cookies that I made last night when I couldn't sleep."

Tag approached Chani two hours later, Ayron's hand tight in his. They were needing to leave, Tag wanting to head to Ronan's to look after his farm.

"Chani? We're heading for Ronan's. What can we do for you?"

Chani shrugged, her eyes on Tag. A frown appeared on her face.

"Who's taking care of his farm? Someone has to."

"I'm heading here for tonight and tomorrow. His neighbours will help out as they can. His mom and dad are back from their trip. His dad has worked with him before." Tag's hand went out as Chani staggered, relief on her face.

"Thank you, Tag. I was so worried about that." Chani rubbed at her face. "Where is he?"

"We don't know, Chani. He has just disappeared."

Chani walked through her apartment that night, Eilis watching from her seat on the couch. She had refused to leave her sister, knowing that she would just order her to leave if she asked.

"Chani? What can we do to find him?" Eilis' quiet word broke through Chani's troubled thoughts.

Chani spun, fear flickering across her face for a moment. She had forgotten that her sister was still there.

"I forgot that you were here. That's not good." Chani sank into her easy chair, wrapping her arms around a favourite pillow.

"No, it's not good. You need to be alert and aren't." Eilis tucked her feet up under herself, her head leaning on her hand.

"No, it's not good." Chani blinked rapidly, tears threatening to break loose. She knew that if she started to cry, it would not stop. "I don't cry."

"I know that. We cried enough when Mom and Dad died. What can I do for you?" Eilis watched her sister closely, a sad smile on her face.

"I really don't know. I want Ronan back, safe and sound. I just don't know if that will ever happen. It's not fair, Eilis."

"I know. It's not fair to him. And it's not fair to you. I can see that you are falling in love with him and he with you." Eilis shook her head as her sister's mouth opened to protest. "It's happening, sis. Whether you want it or not, he's your heart. He's the one that I can remember Mom and Dad praying for."

"They did that, didn't they? And Aunt Ash has continued to do that." Chani grew thoughtful, tamping down the anger that briefly flared. "I'm mad, Eilis."

"I know. So are we. I talked to the other ladies today. They all went through a whole lot of emotions, including anger. God is here with us, sis. You know that. It's hard to trust in times like this."

"It is, very hard." Chani sighed once more, feeling that she had been doing that a lot. "I just don't know what to do."

"What about your work? What has Jake said?"

Chani frowned again before her face cleared.

"I'm to work from home if I want to. Just going in if I need to. And of course, I will go to my clients. He has made arrangements for someone to be with me when I do. This is costing him a lot of money."

"He won't look at it that way. I heard it is Richard and his team that have volunteered to do that."

"Richard? Of course, he would. We will owe him so much."

"No, he won't charge us. He never does for friends. He says God won't let him."

Chapter 20

Two weeks later, Chani could feel the anger once more building inside her. She knew it was wrong but she still felt it. She sighed to herself. This is so not working, she thought. She had continued with her work, finding Jake watching her when she was in the office.

Jake approached her that Friday afternoon, standing in the doorway to her office. He was concerned, he had to admit. Chani was losing weight. Her face was paler than normal with dark circles under her eyes.

"Chani? Just how are you?"

Jake's voice had her jumping, fright in her eyes for a moment.

"Jake! I didn't see you there. You scared me."

"I can see that. Sorry!" He grinned at her before he approached to drop into a chair in front of her desk. "You're not sleeping."

"No, I'm not. I can't. All I can see when I close my eyes is Ronan in a coffin. I can't handle that."

"I didn't realize it was that bad. I thought you would be having nightmares. What can we do to make it easier for you?" Jake watched with compassion as she struggled with her emotions.

"I don't know, Jake. I honestly don't know. We've been looking for him. All of his friends and my family have been working on this. Frank has had to set

—

it aside. There is just not enough information to find him or whoever it was that took him." She looked up at him, anger on her face. "I want this over, Jake. I want to know who it is that has done this. And I want to know if it's me or Ronan."

"I can see that, Chani. Listen, Amy asked if you wanted to come over tonight for supper. No strings. Just a time to decompress for a couple of hours."

"Thanks, Jake. I would but Darbi had asked if I could meet with them. Why don't you and Amy join us?"

Jake grinned, shaking a finger at her.

"Not tonight. Elly is sick and we need to be at home. Another time, though, if that works."

"It does." Chani sighed as she stood, her backpack in her hand. She reached for her jacket, a frown on her face. "Jake? There's something different about this. What?"

Jake was on his feet, a stern look on his face. He reached for her jacket, finding a letter tucked into a pocket.

"This. Did you put it there?"

Chani shook her head.

"No. I have not seen that before. What is it?" She reached for it, taking it from him. She opened the envelope, peering into it. "What is this?"

Jake looked over her shoulder and frowned.

"That's Ronan's watch. This is strange, Chani." He looked at her, finding her frowning at him.

———

"Does this mean that Ronan is still alive?" Hope was rising in her.

"It might." Jake turned as he heard footsteps. "And here is Ronan's father. Ian, have you any word?"

Ian shook his head, fatigue weighing him down. He had been working Ronan's farm with help but it was still physical labour that he was not used to.

"No, not a word. I was hoping to have him home by now." He slipped down into a chair, his legs suddenly not able to hold him upright.

Chani was on her knees beside him, concern on her face. She had appeared at Ronan's farm a few days after he had disappeared, dressed to work there. Ian had met her, a puzzled look on his face until she explained who she was. He and Meg, Ronan's mother, had taken her to their hearts, having heard from Ronan about her. There had been a tone in his voice when he had talked about her that they had waited to hear.

"Ian? Are you okay? No, you're not. Don't tell me that you are. I can see that you're not." Chani glared at Jake as he laughed. "It's not funny, Jake."

"No, it's not, Chani, but you are. You are taking care of everyone again even though you need that yourself."

"Well, someone has to." Her disgruntled tone had a smile appearing on Ian's face that he quickly covered as she turned back to him.

"I'm fine, Chani. Just tired for a moment. You're not, though." He watched her closely, just wanting to gather her up and take her home to Meg.

Only, he couldn't do that. She had her own family to turn to.

"I'm okay, I think, Ian. It's just this." She showed him the envelope.

Ian took it, his eyes on her before he looked into it. Drawing in a deep breath, he prayed for his son.

"This is Ronan's. His grandfather gave it to him when he graduated Grade 8. Dad passed away before Ronan made it into Grade 9, very suddenly. He never parts with it." Ian looked up, a devastated look on his face. "What is meant by this?"

"Someone wants us to know that they have him."

"But is it the men who took him or someone who is keeping him safe?" Chani's question had the two men turning towards her.

"Why ask that, Chani?" Jake was troubled by her question.

"It's just that I don't think Ronan is in the hands of evil. I don't get that when I am praying. I think that he is safe somewhere but has been hurt. Whoever it is has done this to let us know that he is safe. Only, how did it get into my jacket?"

Jake stared at her before he was reaching for the phone, a call into their security company, a request for them to search the feed from that day.

"Someone was in here, Chani. We need to find out who."

"That scares me, Jake. I could have disappeared again."

"Yes, you could have. From now on, we lock the doors. Anyone who comes in has to be buzzed in. Our staff has already asked to have that done. They care for you, Chani, and want this over for you."

Chapter 21

Chani stared at her aunt later that evening. Ashlynn had simply hugged her and then stood back, her hands on Chani's arms. She didn't say anything. She didn't have to.

"Aunt Ash? What is it? Oh, no! It's Ronan! He's dead, isn't he? And it's my fault." Chani reached to cover her face with her hands. She didn't hear Frank behind her.

"No, it's not that, Chani. It's you. What can we do for you?" Ashlynn watched as Chani stared at her and then turned and walked away. They heard the door close behind her. "Did she really just do that?"

Frank nodded, turning to walk after Chani. He didn't see her at all and that worried him. He walked to the driveway and then nodded. Chani had driven away. He reached for his keys and then paused, turning back to the house for a moment. Chani needed time, he knew, but this was not the way to do it. She was shutting out her family just when she needed them most.

Ashlynn stood beside Frank, a hand on her cheek.

"She's gone?" At his nod, she sighed. "She has done this in the past. When I first took them in, she would hide from us, trying to come to terms with what had happened. I thought she was over it."

"She's doing that partly to protect herself. And to protect her family. She's angry. That worries me,

Ashlynn. That's when she'll act without thinking." Frank studied his friend, wishing that his wife was there to talk with her.

"She is. And I'll need to address that with her. I can't let her do that."

"Ashlynn, wait. Let me talk to someone who can help. She and her husband went through some pretty serious stuff before they married. She has always offered to talk to anyone going through stuff like this."

"She would? That would be wonderful."

"She's a friend of Abe and Emma's. I'll reach out to her tonight." He groaned as his phone chimed. He squinted at it and then grinned. "I don't have to reach out. Darci has reached out to me. I'll call her later and ask that she call Chani. A cold call might work."

Ashlynn snorted, bringing a wider grin to Frank's face.

"It might but it might backfire on you, you know."

"That it might." He sent off a quick text to Darci with Chani's name and phone number, a brief explanation attached. "She'll call her over the next day or so and come here if she feels that she needs to. Don't worry. Her husband is an officer."

"He is? Okay. What has Emma had to say?"

"Not a lot. She's working through it but has other investigations on the go. Evan and Shea work for her and have been putting in time on this as well. I expect that they'll be around sometime over the next couple of days, even if just to tell Chani that they are working it."

"Tag has a wonderful group of friends. The ladies have been calling us all, just to talk and pray for us."

"That's what Tag has said. I've had a long talk with him, just to see what he could tell me."

"And I won't ask. Not if it involves any information that would find Ronan. We need to do that. We need that for his parents and for Chani."

"How close are those two?" Frank had his own suspicions on that.

"I really don't know. Chani usually tells me just about anything, but not this. That tells me that she is thinking through and praying through this. Only she is scared that Ronan won't come home."

"He'll come home, Ash. It just not be the way that we are praying. We have to prepare ourselves for that."

Ashlynn nodded, a sober look on her face. Frank had just expressed her thoughts. Those thoughts did not sit well with her but she knew that they were only too true. She had lived through sudden death with her brothers and their wives and knew just the devastation that they could face.

"I'll call her later." Ashlynn made a move to turn to return to her home but stopped as Frank's hand rested on her arm.

"Let one of the other girls do that. Send her a text that you love her and are worried about her.

Include one of your verses for her. She's hiding right now. They do that for those they consider parents. To Chani? You've stepped in as a parent to her over the years. It's not the relationship that you ever thought you would have with her, but it is what God willed."

"He did that, didn't He, Frank? There have been many times that I just wanted to run away and live somewhere no one knew me. But the girls needed me. I set aside my own plans and dreams for them."

"And they will never forget that. There is still something that bothers me, though. Why the music box?"

"That. Why that? I didn't realize that it had disappeared. Given that, I have no idea what else was taken that we don't know about. The girls not likely will remember after all these years."

Chapter 22

The next day, Chani stared at Frank before shaking her head. There is no way that what he was saying was true. How could it be?

"I don't understand, Frank, just what it is that you are saying. And besides, you're not working today. You're off, aren't you?"

Frank grinned at her, mischief in his eyes for a moment.

"No, I'm not working but the chief did ask me to speak with you. He's very worried about you and Ronan."

"He shouldn't be. And just where is Ronan? Are you any closer to finding that out?"

Frank nodded, for once relief in his mind.

"We have a good idea where he is. Someone who knows where he is has reached out to us. And no, I can't tell you. We need to go in and find him and bring him home. We need to talk with him and get his statement before you or his parents speak with him."

"I know that, Frank. I do know that." Chani's anger flared before she shook her head. This situation was causing her anger to grow and she disliked that. She was praying daily for that anger to leave. Only it wasn't.

"It's okay to be angry, Chani. All victims do go through that at some point."

"That's what a Darci said. She called me this morning. I didn't know who she was until she told me.'

"Darci called? That's good. She's a forensics psychologist but she is also a victim. She knows to a certain degree what you are facing."

"She told me her story. It's brutal. I pray that doesn't happen to us." Chani paced before she spun, tramping back towards Frank. "Where do we go now, Frank? How do we find these people? And before you say anything, I know there is more than one party involved. There has to be. Ronan wouldn't have known of Mom's music box. So for someone who is after him to send it to me? That doesn't happen."

"No, that didn't come from those men. It came from someone else. And that someone is not a person who we are able to track down readily. That worries me."

"Me, too. I am just afraid that Darbi, Eilis, or Aunt Ash will be harmed.'

"That's always possible. We're trying our best to find out who, Chani. But whoever it is has been keeping themselves hidden."

"I think it's a woman. Don't ask me why, but that what's I think."

"It may well be. We have seen that before. Now, other than the watch being sent to you, have you received any other material, letters, text messages, photos?"

Chani shook her head.

"No, I haven't. I don't know if Ronan has been. Ian hasn't said anything." Chani frowned at Frank, feeling that frowning was all that she seemed to be doing lately. "Jake said he's locking the office when I'm there. That's not fair to anyone else."

"But it is, Chani. That keeps all of you safe. Someone may be hurt by whoever it is after you. That's a possibility we have discussed with Jake and everyone else in the office. Richard has agreed to find someone to be with you when you are out on your travels. That will help. We need to watch out for your clients as well."

Chani paled, realizing that Frank had gone somewhere that she had been ignoring.

"They are in danger too, aren't they? I should just quit my job.'

"And by doing that, you might be playing into their hands. There has to be something that ties you and Ronan together, other than both of you working in the occupations that you do."

"But our occupations are not connected. At least, I don't think that they are."

"They're not." Frank stared down at the keys which he had pulled from his pocket. "I can't emphasize enough, Chani, that you need to be cautious."

"I'm tired of being cautious, Frank. That is not bringing whoever it is out into the open where you can find him or her."

"Don't do anything rash, Chani. I don't want to explain to your family if you get hurt or killed." Frank stared her down before he walked away.

Chani sighed to herself once more. Frank was right, she knew. She had to be careful. Only, she didn't want to be. She wanted to be out there, looking for Ronan and finding him.

Eilis stood beside her sister, having tucked herself away as Frank was talking with Chani. She had come by the night before, not saying anything, just being there. The sisters were close, drawn closer by their shared sorrow.

"Chani, what are we missing? Have we looked at your clients?"

Eilis' quiet question had Chani turning towards her.

"You know, I don't think that we did. Now, we need to. Who is available that can help?"

"Brinn and Gareth are away. Darbi had a meeting to be at. Aunt Ash? She's working at the sale at the church." Eilis chewed at her lip even as a knock came at the door. "Where you expecting anyone else?"

"No, I wasn't." Chani pulled the door open to stare at the two couples standing there. "Shea and Breckon. The manager let you in, didn't he? And who do you have with you?"

Shea grinned at her even as Breckon hugged her.

"You are correct. He did let us in. He saw us coming and knew that you were home. He's very worried about you, he tells us. And this is Doug and

Darci. Darci tells me that you two spoke on the phone and that she just had to come and meet you."

Chani's eyes were on Darci, not finding her to be quite what she expected.

"Chani? Hi. Forgive us for just walking in on you. This is my Doug. We're here to help you." Darci held up a folder. "I have some stuff here to go over with you. But first, have you eaten? I know I didn't have much of an appetite when we were in danger. Doug's Uncle Mac made sure that we ate. And a friend who has an Irish bake shop sent some goodies."

"No, we haven't. Not yet. Frank was here first thing, almost before we were ready to face the day. Now, the kitchen is this way. I'm not sure that I have enough though."

"Chani?" Doug waited until Chani looked around. "Here. We brought food. And I hear tell Richard is heading this way as well. How be I go down and wait for him while you ladies sort out the meal?" Doug was away before Chani could reply.

Chani stared after him, not quite sure what was happening. She turned as Darci hugged r, laughter in her voice as she spoke.

"That's Doug. He's the head of our ETF teams at home. He'll likely take a walk around the building with the manager, assessing it for security. They'll make it as safe as they can for all of the tenants, not just you."

Chapter 23

Watching Chani interact with her sister, Darci nodded. They had a good relationship, given what they had gone through. Darci was afraid for Chani, just knowing what she had been through herself. Almost losing her life had not been part of what she had ever expected.

Doug nodded towards Chani, his thoughts on what she may well face.

"Darci? Have you given her your profile yet?"

"No. I am almost afraid too. And that's not me. I haven't given it to the investigator yet. I need to do that, but I want to have Chani's reaction first."

"That's not you, Darci. What's so different about this?" Shea had approached, Chani with him.

"Profile? What are you talking about?" Chani searched the faces of the ones near her.

"Darci used to work as a forensics psychologist, as she has told you. Part of that was preparing profiles for the perpetrators. She is good, one of the best that I have seen. She only does it for friends now." Doug pointed towards the living room. "Can we sit and let Darci go over it with you? But first we need to pray."

Chani raised her head as they finished, feeling refreshed in her heart. She had needed that, she knew. Granted, her family and friends had been praying with her. But to have Doug and Darci pray with her, strangers until today? That blessed her more than she could express.

"Thank you, Doug. Darci. Now, what is it that you have for me?" Chani's turned her attention to Darci.

"This." Darci lifted up a folder. "This is a profile of who we think is after you and Ronan. And somehow, you two have connected before all this started. As to why that is?' I do not have a clear picture of that as yet."

"How do you do this?" Chani was intrigued. She had never met anyone like Darci before.

Darci shrugged, not quite sure how to respond.

"I don't know, Chani. It's a gift from God. There was a time that I hated it, regretted that I could do it. God worked through me to solve what Doug and I went through. And since then, I have used it for friends and the odd other case." She looked up at Doug, finding him watching Chani closely. They would talk later, she knew, and he would give her his assessment of the situation. "Now, as to the culprit. You have two different parties after you."

"I know. I don't like it." Chani's disgruntled remark brought laughter to the room. "So, who is after me?"

"The one after you is clever. He or she is hiding in plain sight, as we say. And that is frightening for you, I would imagine. He or she is older than you, in their forties. They have never truly succeeded in what they have attempted to do. Their parents were, becoming prominent in town, but they failed at everything they have tried. They watched you and Ronan grow and become successful in your careers. They see the quality of your friends and family. They resent the fact that you were as popular as you would allow yourselves to be. They resent every accomplishment that you have achieved. They are trying to come between you and Ronan, trying their best to prevent you from becoming a couple. That is something that they have failed to achieve themselves. They are loners, on the edge of everything they have tried. They have become involved in crime, just because it was there and it was something they became good at."

"That's about what we thought." Eilis spoke up, her eyes on Darci. "What else?"

"I am not sure what else to tell you. You do need to be very careful. They are becoming very vindictive, that is obvious. They have so-called friends who will help them in their task of harming you and Ronan."

"But you said there is someone else. Is that someone who has been sending Brinn and me stuff that belonged to our parents?" Chani was worried about that.

"It is. I don't have a clear picture of that person as yet. I just don't have enough information to do that, but I am working on it."

Doug and Darci left soon after that, leaving the four staring at one another.

"Did she just do that?" Chani was in awe.

———

"She did. She's good. She even better when she can interview the culprit or their family. I would not be surprised to find her sending you more information than this. And she will come up with a profile for what is going on with your parents. It's who she is and what she does best. She has an arts and crafts store now that is doing very well." Richard spoke up.

"Okay. I just don't know who she would mean. I don't remember anyone like that. And if they have been around us, I should."

"They would be careful not to be too obvious, I suspect, Chani." Breckon spoke up. "That's how they do it. They work through others as well. Likely someone that you would accept around you, not thinking that they were dangerous."

Chani nodded slowly, her thoughts troubled. Her mind drifted through the people that she had been in contact with and frowned once more, something that she thought she had been doing a lot lately.

"We're working through my clients and their families. That takes a while I know. But how do I stay safe if it's one of them?"

"That we will work on. Abe has sent me information." Richard had returned, having had to leave for a while. "We'll talk, Chani. We'll do our best to keep you safe. Silver and Naomi will go with you to your clients. Jake is working on getting permission for that. Your clients are concerned about you. I don't know if you know how well liked you are by them. They are willing to wait for you to come if that is necessary."

"They are? They are so special, I would hate to do that. They need the continuity of me being there every week."

"They know that, Chani. All are willing to have you call them or do a video call with you if that is what it takes. They are not concerned about their plants. They are concerned about you."

Chani sat back, mulling over Richard's words, her heart warmed by them. She knew her clients were special. She just didn't know that they had felt like that.

Chapter 24

Her feet moving as quickly as they could, Chani ran for her office, struggling to unlock the door and then slamming the door behind her. The door locked automatically, something that Jake had changed. She stared at the door, a hand over her mouth, hearing the door violently tugged at. The lock held, and she breathed a sigh of relief.

A sound behind her had her spinning, a scream torn from her. Jake stared at her and then at the door.

"Chani?"

"They chased me, Jake. I almost didn't make it into the office." Chani spun back to stare at the door. "They were that close to me. I didn't see them when I parked."

Jake reached for the phone in that area, calling for help. He turned to Chani, finding her shuddering in fright. He simply shoved her into a chair and then reached for a hot drink for her.

"Here, Chani. An officer is on his way. They will let Frank know as well." He reached for her jacket and backpack, taking them to her office. When he returned, Jake simply stood and watched her.

Frank set his phone done on his desk, his eyes on the work waiting for him. It disturbed him that someone had tried to nab Chani that morning. However, he could not had seen it coming that way. Not just yet, he thought.

Chani paced her office, unable to concentrate. The officer had not been able to find the men, but their footprints were obvious in the light covering of snow that had fallen overnight. He was unable to tell her who had been after her or if they were still in the area. That was not obvious.

Jake approached Chani's office, watching her pace.

"Chani? Where do you want to be?"

Chani shrugged, her eyes hooded.

"I don't know. I'm just dangerous no matter where I am."

"Not necessarily. We're working with the police to keep you and the rest of us safe. If you are out on your own somewhere, not at work, how do you stay safe?"

"I don't. I just go do what I need to. I don't pay attention to those around me." Chani was angry once more, something that she felt she had been living with for months. "And that could mean I disappear or die. I know that."

"That's it exactly. Do you have any idea who?" Jake watched as she struggled with herself before she said a name. He stared at her before he nodded. "Him and his brother. They have always tried to make inroads into the town but no one has let them. There have always been rumours about them."

"There has been? I didn't know that. I wish I had. I would have gone after them." Chani reached for her jacket and backpack. "I need to leave, Jake. I just can't work today. This has rattled me."

"That it has. Let me have your keys. I'll bring your car close to the building. And someone will follow you home." Jake walked to the back door, shoving it open, and hitting the unlock button on the key fob. The explosion that followed slammed the door into him, driving him backwards and to the floor.

Chani screamed and ran for him, other office staff reaching to call for help. Jake shook his head, sitting up as Chani dropped to her knees beside him.

"Jake? What happened?"

"Your car." He struggled to speak, the breath knocked from him. "Your car. It just exploded."

"Exploded? Just how did that happen?" Chani was on her feet, shoving open the door, to stand just inside the building and stare at the burning hulk that was her car. "My car!"

"Your car, Chani." Jake reached around her to pull the door close. "And no, you are not going out there. That's what they are waiting for. You step out that door? You disappear. And we would have no way of knowing where you are. If you had been the one to hit the key fob, you would have been seriously injured or killed."

Frank walked through the office, searching for Chani. This had just taken a turn that he had prayed would not happen. Her life was now at risk. And he knew Chani well enough to know that she would first hide from her family and then go on the offensive, not caring if she was harmed.

"Chani?" Frank watched as Chani stiffened without turning around. She continued to pour her coffee and then one for him. "We need to talk, Chani. This has just gone to another level. They don't care if you're killed. And we still don't have a definitive reason why."

"I wish I had never come here. So many people are being affected by this. So, Frank, tell me. Is this related to Ronan and me or my parents?" Chani turned around to face him, a hard look on her face. She didn't take in the soft blue of the walls or the comfortable furniture that Jake had chosen for their break room.

"We don't know that yet, Chani. Our work with this has just started. It could be related to something totally different."

Chani's face darkened.

"I don't want to hear that, Frank. I want this over and over now."

"We understand that, Chani. Only that won't happen. You know that as well as I do. Now, you'll tell me exactly what happened today. Don't leave out one little bit of information. That may well be what we need to solve this."

Chapter 25

Ashlynn stared at Chani, a hand over her mouth, as her niece moved around her kitchen. Chani had not wanted to go home, instead heading for her aunt's, praying that she would be at home. Ashlynn had been, a rare day off during the week for her, taking accumulated overtime.

"Chani? What happened? What did you just say?"

Chani shrugged. Now that she was away from the office, it didn't seem real what had happened.

"Someone chased me into the office. Jake was going to drive me home and when he hit the key fob for my car, it exploded. Frank was there. He's not sure who it was."

"No, he wouldn't. Not yet, anyway. Now, what are we to do with you? How safe are you going to be until we find these people?"

"I don't know, Aunt Ash. I am scared. No, terrified is how I would describe it." Chani refused to look at her aunt, jumping as she felt herself in a hug.

Ashlynn's prayers rose for her niece, feeling her calming down as the prayers sank in. She didn't release her right away, knowing that Chani needed her hug. Of all the girls, Chani had always been the one needing the most hugs. She had been like that all her life, Ashlynn realized.

"Aunt Ash? How do we do this? How do we find the ones responsible? I can't go on like this. I am putting so many people at risk." Chani's composure broke and she began to weep, finding Ashlynn's hug tightening around her.

"I don't know, love. I really don't know." Ashlynn wiped at her own tears, not the first that she had wept for her girls. "Here. Let's get our coffee and go to my office. Emma has sent on some material that I have not had a chance to look at. Let's do that. The other girls are heading here after work. Gareth said his parents were too. I know Garrett has been looking into this for us, working with Emma on it."

"He has? He shouldn't be."

"But he will. He considers us all family, you know that, Chani. It's what they do for family."

Chani stretched on the couch, her eyes closing as she prayed. She continued to keep her eyes closed when she finished, hearing the faint sounds of her aunt moving around. She slept, her body needing that.

Ashlynn stood for a moment before she reached for a blanket to cover her. Her hand rested on Chani's hair as she prayed for her. Yes, she thought, God is here. He does protect and heal and lead. This time, it is difficult to trust.

Four hours later, Ashlynn turned as she heard the door open and close and then footsteps approaching her. Gareth and Brinn were there, Garrett and Meg with them.

"Aunt Ash? You're white! Why happened?" Brinn moved to hug her.

"Chani is sleeping and has been for a number of hours. She had an incident this morning. Someone tried to grab her on her way into the office and then her car exploded." She shared a look with Garrett, who simply nodded and moved away, heading for the office that she had told him to use. His phone was out to call Frank.

Brinn paled as Gareth wrapped her in his arms. This was worse, he thought, than some of what they had faced.

"She's okay?" Brinn turned her head, not hearing anything from the living room.

"I really don't know. Frank was there, she said, but she's not saying much. But this did make her weep. And that's not her."

"No, it's not. But how can we help her?" Gareth reached to take the tray from Ashlynn, heading for the living room.

"That I don't know. We are working in the dark here, Gareth. I wish I did know what we could do. The only thing that we can do is pray. And that we are doing."

"That we are, Ashlynn. Now, let's eat and then pray. I do have something that I need to speak with you about. Only, I won't have all the information that I need tonight."

"We can do that, Garrett." Ashlynn gently shook Chani awake. "Wake up, Chani. We have food and you need to eat."

Chani sat up, shoving her hair back, her eyes shadowed. She searched those who were there, a small sob suppressed because Ronan wasn't. She had been dreaming that he was free and there with her. Only, her dream was wrong. And she didn't know how she could or would handle that.

Chapter 26

Two weeks or so previous, Ronan had been abducted from his home and taken away. He had had no idea where he was when he walked away from the building that he had been locked into.

The man who had found him watched him closely over that night. He had had a fight on his hands, Ronan beginning to run a high fever. A cough had developed. This had worried the man, Simon by name, who had tried his best to fight the fever with what he had on hand. That had not worked and the fever had risen.

Simon had finally risen just before the son rose and reached for his phone. He desperately needed help and only one person could help.

"John? Are you working today?"

"No, I'm not. What's up?" John Thompson, his brother, worked as an Emergency Room physician.

"I found a young man who was lying in the road. He was soaked through. He's running a very high fever and has a cough. I don't have what I need to treat him. Can you help?"

"I can. You're at home?"

"I am. I'm worried about him, John. And before you ask, I don't have a name on him. He didn't have any identification on him."

"That's okay. I'll grab what I need and head your way. Mary's off as well. What else is wrong?"

"His wrists are cut up some. He had cloth wrapped around them, not bandages. I wonder if he had been a prisoner or something like that."

There was silence at the other end of the phone. John thought it through before he nodded to himself.

"It is likely, then, that he was. We'll be there shortly. Is there anything else that you need?"

"Something for broth and some juice, I think. You know best what to bring."

"I do. Stay safe, Simon."

Simon Thompson turned once more, his eyes on the clock. It wasn't even dawn yet and he was ready to sleep. Only he wouldn't be able to. He had a young man to take care of. And he had to figure out just who he was. That would be difficult, he knew. He walked towards the bunk, a hand out to feel at Ronan's forehead. The fever was rising, he could tell. Simon reached to wring out another cold cloth, replacing the one on Ronan's head.

An hour later, he turned to the door, watching as John and Mary walked towards him. John had a box in his hand, Mary some bags.

"Simon? What have you gone and gotten involved in?" Mary reached to hug him before heading for the kitchen.

"I have no idea, Mary. All I did was find a young man on the road. I had been following him for a while, just not sure what was going on with him."

John nodded, knowing his brother's heard.

"Let's take a look at him." John headed directly for Ronan, setting down the box on a nearby table.

John stood back thirty minutes later, worry on his face.

"He's in rough shape, Simon. Where again did you find him?"

"About a mile from here. I had been watching him for a while before I moved in. He was lying on the side of the road, not moving. He had been there for a while, I think. His clothing was soaked through. He has not roused at all, not all night." Simon was equally worried.

"I'll start an IV and then push some antibiotics and pain medications. Just pray that he doesn't have an allergy to anything." John was as good as his word, standing back when he had finished. His hand reached for Ronan's wrist and then his stethoscope was to Ronan's chest. They had a fight on their hands, he decided. This young man really should be in the hospital, but he didn't think that he would make it that far.

"John?" Mary's hand rested on his back. "How is he?"

"He's in rough shape, Mary. I can't tell you anything but the truth. He may not make it. And we have no idea who he is."

"That is strange, John. He sounds like one of those of our friends who had an adventure."

John turned to look at her, finding her watching him in turn. His eyes then lifted to Simon, who was watching them, a puzzled look on his face.

"Simon, you know those young friends of ours? The ones who were in danger? Mary thinks that your young friend sounds like them."

"She does, does she? And if he is? How do we find that out?"

John shook his head before he felt Mary's hand on his. He looked down, seeing his phone in his hand.

"Good idea, Mary. Then I can go to Caleb or Frankie and see if they can help." He was as good as his word. "I'll drop by and see one of them later today. Now, let's see if this works for him. We've a fight on our hands."

Chapter 27

The day was longer than Mary had expected. She and John had worked together until early afternoon, when John had had to leave. At that point, Simon took over to help. It was out of his line of work, he knew; the work that he had retired from had been as a lawyer. He had been enjoying his retirement, although he was missing his wife who had died a year before.

"Mary, how is he now?" Simon was still worried about Ronan.

"About the same, Simon. He's not getting any better but he is not any worse. John will be back soon. I pray that he has some answers."

"So do I." Simon walked away, heading for the outside to bring in more logs. He added wood to the fireplace and the wood stove in the kitchen. They were enough to keep the cabin at a comfortable level.

John hesitated as he pulled to a stop in front of Simon's cabin. He had spoken with Frankie, a friend but better than that, a detective on the Riverville force. Frankie had not known of anyone missing in their area but had taken a copy of the photo. He had promised to look into it but could not make any promises.

Shutting the door quietly behind him, he didn't hear any sounds but was not concerned. He knew his brother was quiet and Mary would likely be with Ronan, just doing what she did best, nursing him.

Mary turned as she heard John's footsteps, reaching for his hug and then turning back to Ronan.

"How is he, love?" John shed his jacket and cap, dropping them onto a nearby chair.

"About the same, John. His fever is down a little but he's still coughing. His chest is very raspy."

"I feared that. Let's see what we can do." John listened to Ronan's chest and then stood back. "We need a miracle here, Mary. I don't know what I can do for him. I have oxygen in the car. That will help." He turned to head for his car, finding Simon there with the oxygen tank. "Thanks, Simon. Let's get this set up. We're far enough away from the fires that I think we'll be okay."

"Can we move him to my room? We can close the door and that will help."

"Sure." John and Simon worked to do that, Mary helping to settle Ronan once more.

John walked away at last, rubbing at his neck. He was not sure that they were doing the right thing, but he had felt they had no choice. If he didn't get any better, then he would have to take him in to the hospital. That move could kill him, John knew, and that he wanted to avoid

"What did you find out, John?" Mary set a plate of food on the table for him. John nodded and sat, fatigue driving through him.

"Not a lot. Frankie had not heard of any missing men from this area. He's going to look into it, reaching out to other forces if he doesn't hear anything. The only thing is that we don't know if he's on the run from some other province."

"And that he could well be." Simon sat heavily, fatigued. He needed to sleep but was hesitant to in case he was needed.

"Eat, Simon, and then get some sleep. I'm staying over night and tomorrow. Charlie will cover for me. He's been looking to pick up another shift or two."

John looked up from the book that he was reading early the next morning and then set it aside. He was on his feet, bending over Ronan as the younger man tossed and turned. He moved the oxygen mask and helped Ronan to sip from a glass before he set it aside. The fever seemed to have dropped but it was still higher than John would have liked.

He listened to the muttering that Ronan was doing, unable to make out any words. John then simply prayed for the Great Physician to heal this young man. He knew that was all he could do. Modern medicine would work but only God could truly heal.

Mary stood for a moment beside John before she wrapped an arm around his.

"He was awake?"

John shook his head.

"Not really. The fever is down a bit. Listen, I know you had a nap. I'll go grab some sleep and then be back. Call me if you need me."

Mary nodded, her eyes on Ronan, worried about the young man and his family who would not know where he was.

Early the next morning, Simon stood back from the door, watching as Frankie Brennan walked towards him, shaking off the few snowflakes from his jacket.

"Frankie? Just in time for breakfast. I know that you're here because of John and what he asked you. Let's eat and then pray. That young man needs that."

"How is he?" Frank helped dish up the food, something he had done many times before.

"Not much better, I hate to say. He hasn't been awake. And before you ask, he has no identification on him. No wallet. No cell phone. Nothing to tell us anything."

Frankie nodded, knowing that John had been correct the day before. He ate, listening to the other three talk among themselves. He helped to clear the table and then sat, his head bowed at petitions were raised for the young man whose name was unknown to them.

John shared a look with Simon before he nodded. Frankie had some sort of news, he thought.

"Frankie, what have you found out? And what can you tell us?"

"I have looked through our missing persons' cases, reached out to those towns within an hour of us. We'll need to look further, I think. I just don't know how far to reach out. Caleb and I talked. We're working that way. Going an hour out in a circle just to keep it simple for now. If needed, we'll mass flyer the areas out from there."

"That's what we thought. I just wish I knew who he was. He's young enough to have a lady waiting for him. Maybe kids. And parents at least. As well as friends."

Franke left not long after, having stopped to stare down at Ronan. No he thought, he didn't know him. But he wanted to find out just who he was.

John stayed for two days and then left, leaving Mary to help Simon. He would return in the evenings, bringing more supplies for them to use.

Frankie returned after about a week, no closer to knowing Ronan's name than he had been. There just had been no response and that worried him. He had begun reaching out to other towns, praying that he would have word soon.

"Frankie? Any word?" Simon watched the younger man closely.

Frankie shook his head, frustration evident.

"How is he?" Frankie looked towards the bedroom, wanting to go and interview Ronan and not knowing if he was awake and well enough to even do that.

"He's better but still weak. He hasn't spoken much other than to say thank you. We haven't pushed him to find out his name. We've been leaving that for you. Go on in."

Frankie headed that way, pausing in the doorway to watch Ronan, finding him awake and without the oxygen. That's good, Frankie thought. He's well enough not to have to use that.

Ronan turned in fright as he heard footsteps that he didn't recognize. His eyes slid shut as his head pounded. The lady, Mary he thought her name was, had warned him to watch for headaches.

"Hello. I'm Frankie Brennan, a detective from Riverville. You're near there with friends." Frankie sat in the chair near the bed, his eyes never wavering from Ronan.

"Hi. I'm.." Ronan's voice died away. "I'm sorry. I can't remember my name right now. I'm tired." And with that, Ronan slept.

Frankie watched and then rose. It was about what he had expected. Ronan would be doing that. It was obvious that he would not be questioning him that day.

"Mary? He can't remember who he is?"

Mary shook her head.

"He hasn't been able to. John said that was a possibility. We'll have to wait until he's more along the road to recovery, we think." Mary headed back for Ronan, intent on making sure that he was okay.

Simon stood at the kitchen table, his eyes on the doorway that Mary had disappeared through before he looked at Frankie.

"Frankie? I've put out feelers to friends in towns around here. I know that you have, but sometimes people won't talk to the authorities. We don't know if he was running from someone or involved in a crime gone wrong."

"That's what we don't know. Call me if you get any word."

Chapter 28

A week later, Ronan was up and on shaky legs, heading for the living room. He dropped to the couch, the simple walk more tiring than he thought it would be. He looked around, liking the simply but homey look of the room. He stared at the photo of an oil lamp, with a scripture verse etched below it. It was triggering a memory but he just couldn't think of what it was. His eyes closed for a moment as he took a deep breath and then coughed. John, who had been around earlier that day, had simply told him that he had had pneumonia and needed to recover. That would take time. And did he remember yet who he was and where he was from?

Ronan had shaken his head, not quite sure of his name. He had asked if they had found a wallet or a phone and was surprised when he was told no. That was odd, he had thought. There should have been.

Simon set a mug of broth beside him before he stuffed another log on the fire. He then sat in his favourite chair, his mug of coffee on the small table beside him. He watched Ronan carefully. It had been two weeks since he had found the younger man. They were no further ahead, he thought, to knowing why Ronan had been where he was.

"Simon? How do I remember who I am?" Ronan was afraid for someone. Only he had no idea who it was. "I am afraid for a lady, I think. Only I don't know who she is or why I feel that way."

"It's likely a lady who is close to you. Something has made you suppress the memory and that will take time to recover. I have no idea who you are. I simply found you a short distance away from here and brought you to my cabin. John is my brother. He's been in and out over the last two weeks. Mary was here for the first few days until I could manage you on my own."

"Thank you, Simon. Can we pray? Maybe that will help." Ronan closed his eyes, praying for his memory to return and to protect whoever it was that he feared for. He didn't think that it was himself, but he really wasn't sure.

Simon rose at last, heading for the kitchen and returning with the soup that he had prepared for them.

"Eat, son. Then, we'll talk. I'll take notes and see what we can figure out." He grinned as Ronan stared at him, his mouth slightly open. "I was a lawyer until I retired. Once my lady died, I didn't have the heart to continue even though I have kept up my license for now."

Ronan nodded, eating his meal without really thinking about it. He set aside the tray, his eyes once more on the photo.

"That's an interesting photo, Simon. The lamp and the verse."

"It is. My Emily had a friend who believed that we needed to be ready for when Christ returns for us, just like it says in that parable. But more so, she believed that we needed to be ready to be a witness for Him wherever we are." Simon looked up at a slight sound from Ronan, finding his face pale. "Son?"

———

"I remember. I have a friend who has a lamp ornament. Her aunt had it made for her and her sister and cousins. What have I done? Chani? Please be safe!" His eyes closed as he slumped, the memory too much for him to bear.

Simon was on his feet, his hands reaching to push Ronan back on the couch. He crouched in front of him before he was on his feet, heading for a wet cold cloth and water.

Ronan roused as he felt the cold on his face. Fear had him looking around, looking for his captors. He shot a look at Simon, his eyes huge.

"Who are you? Where am I?"

"It's okay." Simon held his hands up. "You're safe. I'm Simon. You've been here in my home for the last couple of weeks, really sick. I found you near here."

"I need to go home. I need to find Chani. She's in danger." Ronan was becoming more agitated as he spoke. His eyes shot towards the door as he heard a knock and then the door opening.

Frankie stood there, not quite sure just what he had walked into. His eyes moved towards Simon, who shook his head.

"This is Frankie. He's a friend, but he is also a police detective here in Riverville. How be you tell us your name and where you're from."

"I'm Ronan Rafferty. And I'm from Evans. How far is that from here?"

"About two and a half hours. That doesn't explain why you're here." Frankie's notepad and pen were out.

"I was kidnapped and brought here. Only I didn't know where I was brought to. I couldn't see anything or speak. I had a blindfold and gag on and my hands were tied behind me. They left me in a building. I was able to stand and cut the rope with a nail. Then I walked out. I don't remember anything past that."

"You were really sick, Ronan. You almost died." Frankie didn't pull his punches when he spoke. "And now we need to know why. Can you tell me what happened?"

"I was in my fields and then someone tackled me. That's when I was taken to some vehicle. They just drove around for hours. I need to get home. I have a farm that I need to be working." Ronan was becoming more agitated as he spoke.

"We'll have John look you over. Tomorrow, I'll head that way with you. Not tonight. Tonight, I reach out to your town's force and see what I can find out. Now, who are you worried about."

"Chani. She and I were abducted weeks ago. Someone is after her. We just don't know why." Ronan didn't look up at that, missing the start that Frankie gave. Simon didn't miss it and wondered that.

"That's okay. We'll figure it out." Frankie rose at last and walked away, needing to call Doug. Doug had mentioned a Chani in passing when they had spoken a few days ago. "Doug?" Frankie didn't hesitate to call him. "That Chani you mentioned? Where is she from?"

"Evans. Darci and I met with her a few days ago. "Why?"

"Did she mentions someone named Ronan?"

"She did." Doug's voice died away. "He's the one with Simon. Why didn't we connect that?"

"We had no reason to. We didn't know that was where he was from, now did we?" Frankie slid behind the wheel of his car, starting it and waiting for heat to start. "Are you working tomorrow?"

"No, I'm not. Why?"

"I'm heading that way tomorrow with Ronan. I would appreciate it if you could come."

Doug stared at Darci as she listened to the conversation, nodding at the question he mouthed to her.

"Darci's free as well. She's willing to go with us."

"She is? Good. I'll leave early in the morning, or as early as I can. It depends on how Ronan fares over night."

Chapter 29

Frankie slowed his car to make the turn towards Ronan's farm. He had been surprised when he found out Ronan's occupation but knew that he shouldn't have been. He shot a glance at the younger man, finding his head back and his eyes closed. A glance at Doug found Doug nodding at him.

Ronan's head raised as he felt the car stop, his eyes opening. He blinked rapidly, trying to clear the blurriness. He was home, and for that, he was thankful. He shoved open the door, standing and hanging on until he could find his balance. Ronan knew that Doug stood beside him, a hand out to help him.

A sound had him raising his head and he frowned.

"Dad? You're here? I thought that you and Mom were away."

Ian moved in to hug his son, holding on tightly, fighting his tears.

"I'm here, son. Mom and I have been here for a while now. Looking after your place. Let's get you inside."

"No, I need to do my chores." Ronan turned to head for the barn, stopping as his head spun. His eyes closed against that feeling, willing it to stop.

Ian frowned at Frankie, who simply shook his head. Their hands were out to help Ronan walk towards the house. His head raised as he heard a female voice as he entered the house.

Meg stood, hands over her mouth, shocked to see her son. She moved forward, wrapping him into her arms, sobs shaking her body.

Darci moved past them, heading for the kitchen to drop the bags that she was holding. Ian appeared, wiping at his eyes, a question on his lips.

"I'm sorry. I don't think that we have met."

"I'm Darci Foster. The tall one who was helping you? That's my husband, Doug. The one who was driving is Frankie Brennan. Both of them are officers in our town of Riverville."

"Riverville? He has been that close?" Ian stared at her, not sure that he had heard her correctly.

"That close. But he has been very sick. A doctor friend of ours helped. His brother was the one who found your son and looked after him." Darci smiled, sadness on her face for a moment. "He can talk. Frankie did get his statement. Now, what can I do for you?"

Ian shrugged, turning as he heard Meg heading his way.

"Meg?" He held her as she walked into his arms.

"Ian? Where has he been? He looks horrible."

"He was very sick, Mrs. Rafferty." Frankie spoke from behind her. "In fact, the physician who was looking after him wasn't sure that he would make it. He'll need to see his own doctor. There is an investigator involved here?"

"There is. I'll call him." Ian moved away, pausing. "Chani!"

"We need to call her. Although she did say that she would be here this morning." Meg moved towards the door, hearing another vehicle. She walked towards the car, finding Chani approaching her.

"Meg? Who's here? I don't know that car." Chani felt Meg's arms around her and knew that Meg was trying to control her sobs. "Meg! Please, dear Lord! Not that!"

Meg hugged Chani tighter, controlling her sobs at last.

"He's home, Chani. Ronan is home."

Chani's movements stilled as she struggled to understand.

"He's home? Meg? When?"

"Just now. Some officers from Riverville brought him home. Come, dear. Let's get you to him."

Chani didn't remember the walk into the house or being introduced to Frankie. She didn't remember greeting Doug and Darci. Instead, her eyes were searching for Ronan. She moved towards him, finding him sitting on the couch in the living room. She sank down beside him, a hand to his face.

Ronan jumped as he felt a hand on his face. His eyes shot open and he stared around, trying to find the men who had kidnapped him. His movements stopped as he saw Chani sitting beside him.

"Ronan? You're home!" Chani was afraid that he wasn't, that it was all a dream that would disappear when she awoke.

"Chani? You're okay?" Ronan's voice was still rough from his illness.

"I am, but you're not." Chani watched him closely, seeing the damage that had been done by his illness.

"Chani! I was so afraid that they had you." Ronan simply swept her into his arms, holding on tight as she sobbed. "They want something. Only they never said what."

Chani rose at last, watching as Ronan slept. His fatigue was obvious. She turned as she felt an arm around her.

"Darci? You're here?"

"I am, Chani. Come. To the kitchen. The three men are out in the barns. Frank apparently will be here soon. Now, we need to make some plans. Plans that I hope we never have to use. Richard is here as well and will be in shortly."

"Yeah, Richard. I've been trying to avoid him." Chani was upset that he had been called in.

"Yes, Richard. He needs to be here. And this stops, Chani. You are in danger as is Ronan. What happened in the last few weeks show us that." Frank stood in the doorway to the mudroom.

Chani glared at him before she turned and walked back to the living room, to drop to a sitting position on the floor, her hand on Ronan's face as he slept.

Frank moved to where he could watch her. He knew just how dangerous it was becoming. He had the letters that she had refused to open or read. Chani had bluntly told him to take them and deal with them. He could no longer let her get away with that.

Chapter 30

Ronan walked through his house late that night, seeing the dim lights that his mother had left on. He knew that she had retired but he wasn't sure about his father. Ian turned as he heard his son's footsteps, a mug of coffee set on the table for him.

"Son? How are you feeling tonight?"

Ronan shrugged, slumping down into a chair.

"How's the farm, Dad?"

"It's okay, son. We've managed to keep it going for you. Tag's been around as have your neighbours. They are looking out for you, son. We'll continue that as you continue to heal."

"But, Dad, aren't you and Mom supposed to leave again?" Ronan looked up, hope in his eyes that they wouldn't be.

"No, not at this time, Ronan. We've talked. We need to stay home for now. You need us."

"Thanks, Dad." Ronan stared around his kitchen, taking in the small touches that his mother had added over the years, making it into a home. "I worry about Chani."

Ian gave a brief laugh, worried about that young lady, a young lady who had grown to mean a lot to them.

"She's been out here as she can. She's fighting mad, as Dad would have said. They would have gotten along so well."

"She's mad? Why?" Ronan was having trouble processing his thoughts.

"Because you disappeared and she couldn't find you. Because of all this. She cares deeply for you, Ronan. I have no idea where you two are heading, but I can see her as part of our family." Ian rose, setting his mug in the sink. "Don't stay up too long, Ronan." He paused, not quite sure what else to say. Instead, a hand rested on his son's head as he prayed for him. He walked away, turning at one point to study the young man sitting there.

Ronan sighed, knowing that he needed to head for bed but not wanting to. He didn't want the dreams that had been flooding his sleep in the last few days. He snorted. They weren't dreams. They were nightmares. He stared at his wrists, wondering where his watch had gotten to. Lost somewhere, more than likely, he thought. He rose at last, reaching for his phone out of habit. He scrolled through the messages, stopping at the one that Chani had sent.

A softened smile lit his face as he walked towards his bedroom. Ronan set the phone down, changed into his pyjamas and then crawled into bed. Reaching for his phone once more, he read Chani's text. He paused and then sent his own back to her, hearts and flowers attached, and with the word that he loved her.

———

Chani reached for her phone. As late as it was, she had been hoping for a message from Ronan. She had not stopped thanking God that he was home. Her family had been surprised that he was. Facing many questions, she had just shrugged, unable to tell them exactly what happened. She couldn't because she just didn't know herself. She read his text, tears trickling down her cheeks as she saw his words that he loved her. She knew that she loved him. Only, she wasn't sure where that would go.

Chani reached to turn off her bedside light, snuggling down under the covers. A prayer on her lips for Ronan, she slept, this night without any dreams. She didn't see the car that sat near the apartment building, the man's eyes on her apartment, watching as the lights were extinguished for the night.

On her feet early in the morning, Chani squinted at her clock. She was due at clients' homes that morning. She drew in a deep breath, knowing that she didn't want to do that. She just wanted to be with Ronan and couldn't. Reaching for her phone, she scrolled through her messages, smiling at the ones from her family. Her aunt's message caused her to pause for a moment. *No,* she thought, *I am not okay. I don't know that I will be ever again. I know that Ronan is home but I have no idea what we are facing now. And that scares me. I know God is in control. But there are times that I need someone physical here to protect me. God, are You listening to me?*

Her day of work finished, Chani trudged towards her apartment, fatigue weighing her down. She stopped abruptly as she saw booted feet in her line of sight. Fear wafted through her as she lifted her eyes. Breathing a sigh of relief, she glared at Richard.

"Richard? What are you doing here?"

Richard simply grinned at her, turned and walked towards the building with her. He reached for her keys to unlock the building door and then followed her up to her apartment. He unlocked that door and then stared her down before she entered.

"You're searching this, Richard?" Chani was scared and to be scared like that made her angry.

"I am, Chani. This is how it's going to be for now." Richard went through her apartment and then was back with her, handing over her keys. "Now, we need to talk."

"No, we don't. Go away, Richard." Chani stomped away from him, heading for her bedroom, desperate to clean up. She returned to the kitchen to find Richard had prepared soup and sandwiches for them. "I thought that I told you to leave."

"You did. I didn't. We need to talk, Chani. That happens today. Eat and then we pray." Richard hid his amusement at her mutinous look. He was used to those kinds of looks. They were all part and parcel of protecting people who didn't want protection.

Chani slid from her seat, reaching to clean up the mess from their meal. She hesitated to speak, knowing that Richard would not be there if he didn't feel it was really necessary.

"Sit, Chani. We do need to speak. Let's pray first. This is where it gets dangerous for you and

Ronan. Yes, I know that he is home. But he is still not safe. And we don't have enough information on what is going on to know how to properly protect you two."

Chapter 31

Richard walked towards Ronan's house late the next afternoon, Chani with him. His four team members had spread out, providing security. He had felt it necessary. Chani had yelled at him that she didn't want them and then tried to walk away from him. A hand on her arm stopped her. Richard had been somewhat amused at her reaction but wouldn't let her get away with leaving.

Her thoughts troubled and her emotions in a whirl, Chani kept quiet. She wanted to see Ronan but not like this. She felt like a prisoner, even though Richard had been clear that she wasn't. She just didn't have the freedom that she treasured, the freedom to do what she wanted. She had no way of knowing that the threats directed at her and Ronan were escalating. Only no one knew who was behind it.

Ronan stood on his porch, his eyes on his lady love. He had finally acknowledged it to himself. Only he had no idea how she felt. He caught Richard's eye and then frowned. Richard was here for a reason. He could see two men and two women moving around the house. This is serious, he thought. Not just a simple visit.

"Richard? You're here for a reason." Ronan reached to shake his hand before wrapping Chani into a hug. "Come on in. Chani, your family is on their way. Mom and Dad are heading back from town."

Chani hugged him before moving away, searching for just what she wasn't sure. But she needed to find it. Only what she was looking for was peace and resolution of what they were facing. That was not going to happen overnight, she knew. She tried to draw strength from the verses of Scripture that she had memorized and read over and over. Only that wasn't working out so well.

Richard turned as Stephen approached him. He had not entered the house, waiting instead for his team to do their work.

"Stephen, what did you find?"

"About what we expected. The cameras. This." He held up a letter. "This was in the barn. I don't know how it was missed."

"Then it had to be put in here in the last few hours. They have been in and out of the barn until noon, Ronan said. That's when his parents headed for town." Richard rubbed at his neck. "Does he have security cameras?"

"No, and he needs to. Timothy is heading out to get them. They will be installed today."

"Thanks, Stephen. Now, we need to speak with those two."

"Chani will fight you on this, you know." Stephen grinned at the look that Richard shot at him.

"I know. She knows what Brinn went through and what we had to do. She's trying hard to avoid this. She wants it over and now."

"She does. Unfortunately, we don't have a lot of information. I spoke with Frank earlier, when I was in the barn. He didn't give a lot of information that we can use. I'm not sure if it was because he couldn't or just didn't have it."

"I suspect it's that he doesn't have it. There haven't been a lot of solid leads in this. Frank did tell me a couple of days ago that the case would likely have to be set aside unless something broke."

"That's a shame, Richard. What has Emma to say?"

"Not a lot. She's been away with Abe and his team, working across the country on a case that has absorbed most of her attention. She did say that Evan was working it but hadn't gotten too far. Whoever this is? He's hiding well."

"Hiding in plain sight. Let's work it with them, then. See what we can come up with."

Richard nodded, turning to enter the house, hearing Chani's raised voice. He shook his head. She was on a roll, he thought, coming to a stop near the doorway to the living room. Chani and Ronan were faced off across the couch. Ronan was having trouble keeping a straight face, Richard could tell. And Chani was angry. That much was obvious.

"Okay, you two. Enough. Let's sit and talk. Arguing isn't getting you two anywhere."

"Yes, it is. I want to go home, Richard." Chani refused to turn and look at him.

"Doesn't matter what you want, Chani. You're not going anywhere. You're now in our protective care as is Ronan. For now, we keep you two together. That means here as Ronan needs to work his farm. And yes,

Jake is aware of this. He has said that you work from home now most days and the other days, you will work over a video chat with your clients."

"You can't make decisions like that for me. I am leaving." She spun, ready to run by him. She stopped, seeing the look on his face. He expected her to do just that, she thought.

"Not happening, Chani. My team will stop you. As of now, you are not free to walk around on your own. Your life and Ronan's are at stake. So are the lives of your families. Think about that. Can you live with yourself if something happens to them because you refused to cooperate with us?"

Richard's look of compassion halted Chani's words. He was correct, she knew. She just didn't want to let go of control. She needed to keep to her routine. This would not let her.

"I need to go, Richard. Please?" Chani knew that she was begging but couldn't help herself.

"Not happening, Chani. Now, your family is here. I can hear them and Ronan's parents. And Tag is here as well. Stephen has found cameras around outside. And a letter in the barn. We need to discuss this. There is no option at all." Richard grew stern, knowing that he had to. This couple's lives were in his hands and he didn't intend to lose them.

Ronan paled at the words that Richard spoke. He had thought that might happen but had not really expected it. He simply moved to wrap Chani in his arms, pulling her back against him. He nodded at

Richard before he turned and moved Chani to his office.

Chani stood still, shock flowing through her. She had not expected this. Not at all, she thought. Now what happens?

"Chani? Richard is right. We do need to listen to him. This is his line of work, his expertise. Brinn would tell you that. Just listen to him. That's all we ask."

"I know, Ronan. I just don't have to like it. I want my freedom back."

"And you will have it back." Ronan stared around the room, at a loss for once for words. He stared at the book shelves, the desk, the filing cabinet. He felt the wooden floor under his socked feet. It was home but it felt invaded. He disliked that feeling.

Ronan turned as he heard footsteps approaching, reaching for Chani once more. She clung to him for a moment before she moved away. She felt that she was a real danger to him. Only no one could tell them why.

"Richard? What do we have?" Ronan went on the offensive, wanting to know what he could. He simply dropped to a sitting position on the floor, his shoulder touching Chani's leg.

"We need to bathe you two in prayer on a constant basis. Frank is on his way. He says he has an update for you. Which case, he didn't say."

"Which case?" Chani was confused. "I thought that there was only one."

"There are two, Chani." Brinn spoke up, feeling Gareth tighten his arm around her. "There is yours. And there is the one involving our parents. I want both of these solved and yesterday."

Chapter 32

Chani slumped down once more into a chair in the office. Richard had left but his team was still around. She had seen them walking around outside and knew that some were in the house. She had tried to avoid her family. Only that had not worked out so well. Eilis had cornered her, asking her what was going on. Chani had no answer. She didn't know herself.

Garrett had appeared at some point, just when Chani wasn't sure. She had refused to speak with him, just walking away from him. Garrett had nodded. She's running, he thought. Only she's going to run right into problems. He had turned to Ronan, finding Ronan waiting for him to speak.

"Ronan? How are you?"

Ronan had shrugged, not sure how to respond.

"I am really not sure." Ronan had sought a chair, finding himself overly tired. He hated that feeling. He was used to working and working hard. That wasn't an option for him right at the moment.

"That sounds about right. Let me speak with you, leave you what I can. You need to sit Chani down and go over this with her. If she won't listen to me, you, or Richard, then I'll go to Frank."

"I know, Garrett. I know that. She's on the run. It's her nature to go on the offensive. Right now, that can't happen. I fear for her when it is clear who it is. She'll go after them without thinking about herself."

<hr>

"She will. We need to prevent that. Only I don't know that we can. She is free to walk away from this." Garrett studied Ronan, seeing the fatigue that he was trying hard to hide. "You need to get some sleep, Ronan. You're not well yet."

Ronan yawned and then nodded.

"I know that I do. Only I am afraid that Chani will walk away if I'm not awake to stop her." He didn't see Chani stopping in the hallway as she heard his voice.

Chani turned, not sure where to run to. Silver stood there, her eyes compassionate as she reached out to draw Chani back to the office.

"He loves you, Chani. He's afraid that he'll lose you."

Chani nodded, a sober look on her face. She concentrated on her hands, not wanting to see the pity that she was sure would be on Silver's face.

"I know. I just don't want him hurt because of me."

"It doesn't matter, Chani. He'll be hurt if you leave. If you stay, then we have a better chance of keeping you two alive." Silver simply bowed her head and began to pray.

Chani felt herself relaxing as she listened. *She's right, Lord. I'm trying to do this on my own and in my own strength. That never works out. Your way and plans are so much better. I don't know what we face, but You do. You have known since before time began.*

"I get that, Silver. I just don't know how to do this. It was different for Brinn and Gareth. They were a couple already. I don't know that Ronan and I ever would be." She didn't see Ronan hesitating in the doorway. She jumped as she felt arms around her.

Ronan looked up as Silver stood and mouthed a thank you to her. They both needed sleep, Ronan knew, but this needed to be resolved that night. That is, if they could.

Chani heard Ronan's softly whispered prayer and sank back against him. She felt loved and cherished in his arms but she was so afraid of Ronan being hurt.

"Chani? We need to talk. I am not sure if this the time that we would choose, but it seems as if we need to. I love you, Chani, and have for a while. I would like to spend the rest of my life with you, but I'm not sure that we will. I'm just not sure how you feel." He waited, realizing that she needed time to absorb what he had said.

Chani had listened to Ronan baring his heart to her and drew in a deep breath. She was loved and treasured, and that made her happy. But the danger they were in made her hesitate. She turned her head, finding Ronan looking at the floor and not at her. He had a worried look on his face.

"Ronan? Thank you. I wondered if you loved me. I love you too. I just don't want to see you hurt again because of me."

"You do?" Ronan looked up at her and then reached to kiss her. "I love you, darling. We'll get there. We'll find the ones responsible for both situations."

Chani sighed, knowing that he had gone to the root of the problem.

"I know that we will. I just don't see that happening very soon." She was content to be held. "You have an early day tomorrow, Ronan. You're still trying to recover."

He nodded, before he rose and drew her to her feet. He kissed her once more and then watched as she walked away. His heart felt full, but he was so afraid. He had no idea what lay ahead of them but it would be dangerous and life-threatening. He had seen the letter that had been found that day. He had no idea of what that person was asking for. He had no documents, no jewels, nothing of value that was requested.

Richard watched before he too sought his rest, a blanket covering him as he stretched out on the couch. He would be up and down all night, he knew. Silver and Timothy had already retired, leaving Naomi and Stephen on guard. They would switch out after a few hours. It was how they worked.

His thoughts on the letter that had been found, Richard was puzzled. Ronan didn't have that kind of material. He knew that from their conversations. So what were they really after, he questioned. And until they found them, they would not know. That scared him. This put the couple at risk and put their family at risk as well. It also made their work more difficult.

Just how that would work out, he had no idea. But he knew the One who was in charge and he trusted that One completely.

Chapter 33

Chani's heart was racing as she sought for somewhere to hide. Timothy had been with her at the office and had sent her into the building.

"Find somewhere to hide, Chani. Now!" His voice was harsh with his anger, not directed at her but at whoever it was that he had seen.

Timothy had ducked the fist swung at him, his own fist planting itself into the man's face. He didn't hear the steps behind him until too late. He had turned halfway around to meet the threat when a heavy object landed against his head, sending him to the ground. Timothy sprawled seemingly lifeless on the ground before he was hauled to his feet and dragged to a van. Dumped inside, he didn't hear the threats sent his way before two of the men headed for the office, intent on finding Chani.

Chani drew in a shuddering breath, barely able to hold back her sobs. Timothy was in danger because of her. She heard the thudding footsteps heading her way and desperately searched for a hiding place. She didn't find one and instead ran for the back door, hoping to be out of it and to a hiding place.

Hands grabbing her arms roughly pulled her to a stop. She sobbed, begging them to let her go. It was to no avail. A gag was slapped across her mouth before she was dragged roughly from the building and to a vehicle. She was shoved inside, landing harshly on the floor. Her eyes closed against the brief moment of pain that she felt before her wrists were bound.

<hr>

Rough conversation hit her ears but she was too frightened to even try and decipher what was being said. Her eyes opened to a slit and she watched as Timothy just laid still, hardly seeming to breathe.

The vehicle sped from her office site and towards an unknown destination. Chani could not get a sense of direction and that scared her. She tried to relax but fear drove her breath to be uneven, catching in her throat with her sobs.

Jake walked towards the building an hour later, his eyes on Chani's car. She's early, he thought, just like always. He entered the building, a sense that something was wrong flooding through him. He searched but didn't find Chani. Instead, he found her backpack on the floor, her keys flung across the room. He retreated and reached for his phone. She wasn't here, not by the looks of it, and whoever it was that was with her that day? That person wasn't there either.

Frank walked towards the building, a frown on his face. The responding patrol officer met him halfway there, and he stopped.

"No sign of Chani?"

"Not a one, Frank. I've walked through. Her backpack is there. Her keys. Just not Chani. And Richard has been around. Timothy was with her and there's no sign of him either." Jack was worried. Chani was a good friend from high school. He didn't want to see anything happen to her.

"I see. Okay. The techs are on their way?"

"They're here already. They aren't finding a lot, they said."

Frank nodded, having already figured that out.

"You've talked to the others around here?"

"We're in the process of doing that. It would have been just turning light, we think, by the time that she arrived here."

"That would be about right. Chani likes to be in the office early. And the others start working later during the winter. She was supposed to be working from home. What has Jake said?"

"That she had decided that she needed to be in here today. That there were documents that she needed to retrieve before she could work at home. I had warned her to be careful, to only come when others were here."

"That's not Chani to listen. She's always been determined to prove herself. We could never figure that out during school. Unless it has something to do with losing her parents."

"That could be. She is determined to stand on her own feet." Frank sighed. "And Ronan is involved in this now."

"Ronan Rafferty? I didn't know that they were friends." Jack stared at Frank before he nodded. "I can see them as a couple. They would be good for one another."

"They are good for one another. Okay, Jack. Continue with what you're doing. Come see me when you're back in. I want to hear if you find anything."

———

165

"Will do, Frank. God is in control, even if it doesn't seem as if He is."

Jake turned as Frank stopped beside him. Both men were quiet, worry about Chani uppermost in their minds.

"Timothy was with Chani this morning. He had to have been taken out for them to get to her." Jake finally spoke, not sure what had actually happened.

"Chani was here early."

"She was. She wasn't supposed to be. That was not our agreement." Jake was frustrated.

"Chani would have wanted to be in and out without putting anyone in danger, knowing her. Unfortunately, it didn't work out that way. I'll need to see your security tapes."

"Jack asked for them. The company is running copies and then dropping them off for you. Find her, Frank. I don't want any harm to come to her." Jake walked away, seeing Richard waiting for him. "Richard?"

"Jake? What happened? I lost contact with Timothy and tracked him to here." Richard was searching with his eyes, not seeing Timothy.

"He's disappeared, Richard. So has Chani. It looks as if Chani made it into the building but disappeared sgain." Jake was frustrated but more than that highly worried about her.

"Disappeared? That's what we were afraid of. Naomi headed to your security company to find out what she can. What can you tell us?"

"Not a lot. She was here early, earlier than we had agreed to. I can't imagine how Timothy let her do that."

"He would have assessed the risks and thought it was okay. She's been watched that closely." Richard walked away to where Stephen and Silver waited. "They're gone, guys. I have no idea who or where." Richard was worried, more than he had been since he found out Chani was in trouble. "Now, we need to find them. And that is going to be a difficult task."

"And we have to talk to her family and to Ronan." Silver grew pensive. "I just wish I knew who."

"We'll gather at my place, Silver. Work this through. Her family will be there, that much I know. Garrett was heading that way this morning. And Ronan and his folks will as well. Doug reached out with more information from Darci. She's working this."

"And Emma? Is she?"

"She is when she can. Tag has been around today. I spoke with him." Stephen headed for their vehicle. "He'll reach out to his friends. These people won't have a chance."

"But will Chani and Timothy?" Silver spoke, her words echoing each of their unspoken thoughts.

Chapter 34

There had been no sign of the two missing people. Richard had gone to his sources on the streets without any luck. He didn't think that they were in town. He had that feeling that they had been moved to another town. And if that was the case, Richard had no idea of how to find them or where to start looking.

Ashlynn had taken over providing meals for them. She and the girls continued to work but were at his place as much as they could. Doug and Darci had been around, Darci highly disturbed that Chani had gone again. She had added to the profile which she had provided him but it wasn't helping. Not this time.

Stephen was highly worried as well. Their team was not complete, not with Timothy missing. Silver and Naomi weren't saying much, but he knew the worry that they were hiding.

Ronan had been there as much as he could, not shirking his work, but desperate to find the love of his life. He had watched Richard's team before he turned, searching for paper. Stephen had helped him place paper on the walls, a grin on his face for a moment as he did so.

"We always end up like this, Ronan. It helps to visualize what we know and don't know." Naomi had spoken from the doorway to Richard's dining room. They had taken over that room and he had gladly let them. "I have pens, markers, high lighters. Whatever we need to work."

They had worked away that day and into the night, before Richard had stopped them and sent them home to rest. Ronan was back as soon as he could in the morning, Tag with him. Ayron had stayed with his mother and father, working with them on what was needed at the farm.

Ronan stood that day, his eyes on a name. Silver stood beside him, her eyes moving between his face and the paper. Tag stood on his other side, worry on his face for his cousin.

"Tag? What do we know about this person?" Ronan's finger stabbed at the paper, anger growing in him.

"Him? I'm not familiar with that name." Tag studied it and then groaned. "He goes by another name, Ronan. Ryan Gray. Is he the one?"

Ronan nodded, Tag confirming his suspicions.

"He's always been on the edge of things. I can remember seeing him in high school. There were always rumours about him. Nothing that we could confirm though. His father is high in a corporation there."

"He is. A manufacturing company that exports and imports. A good way to cover himself. I heard that he works there as well."

Silver had been listening to them, turning to her laptop and pulling up the programs that she needed. She ran his name, not surprised at what she found or the number of aliases that he had. Richard sat beside her, a questioning look on his face.

"This guy, Richard. He's involved somehow. I need to research him more to see if his father is."

Richard had been reading the documents that Silver had pulled up. He agreed with her assessment.

"Run with it, Silver. I'll be around. I have a conference call coming in that will be about thirty minutes or so." He was on his feet, moving away, leaving Ronan staring after him before he turned to Silver.

"Silver? What was that about?" Ronan took Richard's seat, his eyes on Silver.

"This person? Somewhat of a nasty person, I would say. Now, what can we do for you?" Silver watched with compassion as Ronan struggled. "I had a good talk with Chani one day. She told me about the reason for the lamps that they had. It may be that she is going through this to be the light to someone else, to bring them to God."

Ronan nodded, a sober look on his face.

"That's what I keep telling myself. It doesn't make it any easier." He shifted on his chair, watching Ashlynn as she sat beside him. "Ashlynn?"

"Silver is correct, Ronan. There are times when God allows things and events in our lives. It could be an illness, an accident, a loss of some sort. But He can and will work through us in any situation. We are simply to be a light, to have our lamps ready to witness for him. We need to keep our oil source filled. It is during the difficult times that we struggle the most to do that. All we need to do is ask. God hears our prayers and replenishes us. It does not mean that we don't suffer. It is how we deal with our suffering and difficulties that make us the lamplight for those around us."

"You've put it in a way that I had never thought of. I am so familiar with that parable, but always thought that it was only that we needed to be ready for when Christ returned. But we don't sit idle or sleep while waiting, do e?"

Ashlynn reached to hug him, holding on for just a bit, feeling the lost little boy that he was trying to bury deep inside.

"I am glad that I could explain it to you, Ronan. It is a lesson that I have had to learn and relearn over and over again. It was not easy to set aside my plans and dreams to take in the girls. But there was never any doubt or hesitation that was what I would do. They are my family."

Ronan nodded before he rose, heading for the back porch. He needed some space, and only being outdoors would do for him. He spent so much of his life outside that in times of trouble or worry, that was what he thought.

Doug stood and watched him. He had come back around, Abe with him that time. Abe was closeted with Richard on the conference call. He approached Ronan, a hand resting on Ronan's shoulder for a moment before he stood.

"What?   No words, Doug?"   Ronan was surprised that Doug didn't speak.

———

"No, you don't need words, Ronan. What you need right now is just someone to stand with you. To pray for you. To stand with you. This is where our minister, Greg, would say that we are standing in the gap for our friends. Others did it for Darci and me. When I almost lost her, I thought my life was over. She survived the attack, but it did change her. It changed me."

Chapter 35

Richard moved quietly through his house, searching for his team. Frank had appeared, sent to work with him on the case. He had been deep in research in Richard's office, nodding as Richard had risen and disappeared.

"Silver? Where are Naomi and Stephen?"

"Downstairs in the office there. Do you need them?" Silver turned from the sandwiches that she had been preparing.

"I do. Come with me. I have word and we need to work fast. Abe and his team are on their way back this way. Don's on his way here. He'll stay with group here."

Richard faced his team before his head was bowed and he led them in prayer. When he raised his head, he searched each face. They were hurting because Chani had been taken on their watch. But they were also hurting that Timothy was not with them. That broke their team. Richard frowned, a thought crossing his mind.

"Richard? What if this was staged? To split our team?" Stephen spoke even as he looked at the two ladies and then Richard.

"I think that is a good possibility, Stephen. Now, I have word where we think they are. They are half-way between here and Riverville. Abe is on his way from Riverville. We're heading out as soon as we can."

"Don's heading in?" Naomi's question really wasn't a question but a statement.

"He is. His team will stay here until we return. Let's move, people. We want to be there just as dusk is falling and that's cutting it close."

They stood, watching the house in front of them. Abe stood beside him, his team already heading around the house, moving in to be in position when they were needed.

"Abe? They're here?" Richard kept his voice quiet.

"They are. There are three different guards here. We'll move in but we'll need your team to watch for anyone coming." Abe moved away, heading for each of his team.

Richard nodded to his team before they separated, each to their appointed spots. He had absolute faith in them.

Abe watched closely, pointing to Ian and Murphy as a man exited the building. They moved in quickly, had him on the ground and then handcuffed and bound. He was led away, locked in one of the vehicles before they moved back into place. This was not what they had expected. They waited as dusk was falling, watching as a second man appeared, calling for the first man. This time, Matt and Luke moved in, taking him down and securing him near the vehicles.

Nathanial moved closer to Abe, watching closely.

"That should leave only one, correct?"

"That's what we're told. One of them has to be our informant."

"I pray that he's the one inside but it could be that he's not even here."

"You just had to say that, didn't you?" Abe touched his earpiece, saying the words for them to move in.

The team moved in quietly, careful not to make a sound. They searched the building, not finding the third man, but finding instead a hidden room. On the count of three, the door was broken in.

Timothy looked up through blurry eyes, his head pounding from the treatment when he was taken down. He attempted to rise, not quite making it. Matt was beside him, assessing him. Matt was the paramedic on the team. He turned to Luke, quiet words spoken as Luke helped Timothy to his feet and then away.

Matt turned as he heard Joseph's voice calling to him. He was beside Chani, thinking that he would find her hurt. Instead, he found a lady whose anger seemed to spark off of her. Her eyes were furious. Joseph reached to release her bonds and then her gag.

"Don't say anything, Chani." Matt held up a finger. "We need to get out of here and now."

Chani nodded, on her feet and surging towards the door before they could stop her.

Matt stared after her before he spoke.

"Did she really just do that?"

Joseph gave a quiet laugh.

———

"She did. She is like that, from what Abe has said."

Matt shook his head before he headed after her, almost on a run. They needed to get away and now. They only had limited time to do that.

Sorted out into vehicles, Abe turned to Matt, watching as he assessed Timothy.

"Matt?"

"He's got a concussion for sure, Abe. We need to have him assessed. Their town?"

"No, ours. We need to keep it quiet for now that they're free. County is moving in officers to search the place. They'll come for our two friends."

Richard turned to Chani, finding the same anger brewing just below the surface.

"Chani, were you hurt?"

"No. I'm just so angry. Who were they? They just took me from the office again." She slumped back for a moment, sorrow on her face. "How is Timothy?"

"Timothy is being taken care of. Matt is a paramedic and will look after him. But you?"

"No, I'm not hurt. I just wish they would stop taking me from the office. How am I to get any work done if they keep that up?" Chani turned to stare out into the darkness, leaving Richard's team to exchange glances, Stephen barely able to contain his mirth.

Chapter 36

Chani paced the room that she had been shown to. She knew that it was at Abe's home but it didn't make it any easier to be at peace. She just wanted to go home, to hug her cousins and her aunt, and then to be held in Ronan's arms and told that she was loved. That didn't seem to be happening. Not at the moment. She sighed as she dropped to sit on the bed. *Lord, my attitude needs work. I know that. But this is so frustrating. I don't know who took us or why. Whoever was in charge never showed up. And to keep us tied up like that? Who does that? Please, Lord, let us resolve this quickly. I want to move on with my life and can't.*

Hearing a soft sound at her door, she rose, opening it. Surprised not to see anyone, she felt a hand hit her knee. Looking down, her eyes softened as she dropped to her knees. An adorable little boy stood there, a grin on his face, a little calico cat cradled in his arms.

"Hi, there. You're sweet. Is that your kitty?" Chani grinned at him, reaching to hug him before he shoved back and then handed her the cat. "Oh, I see. You want me to hold her? I can do that."

"Isaac, did you call Chani for a meal?" A lady appeared, causing Isaac to turn and run to her to be picked up.

"I did. She has the kitty."

"Okay then, son. Off you go." She watched as Isaac ran away before she turned. "Hi. I'm Emma. We have met before."

"We have. I just forgot. Where are we?"

"At our place. Don't worry. Frankie will be here soon to take your statements. Then come morning, Richard will head off with you and Timothy."

"Timothy! How is he?" Chani walked beside Emma, heading for the kitchen where she could hear conversation.

"He's sleeping right now. Matt says he has a bad concussion but doesn't think that he'll need to see someone tonight. Here. We have a meal ready. We're not fancy here."

Two hours later, Chani crept into bed, clean and fed. She fell asleep quickly, her dreams filled with Ronan. Her tears dried on her cheeks, unknown to her. Emma tapped at the door and opened it, closing it quietly behind her.

Richard was waiting as she returned to the kitchen.

"She's asleep, Richard. Frankie didn't seem to think that they knew who had taken them."

"I doubt that they did. We're heading out in the early morning, before it gets light. They expect us to wait for daylight. If I could have headed out tonight, I would have."

"No, you need to rest as well. Timothy needs a good night's sleep. And Abe has made arrangements for other vehicles to go with you, just for protection."

<hr>

"I suspect that we'll need it. Thank you, Emma. Now, if you will direct me to a chair where I can sit for the night, I'll head that way."

"In the living room, Richard. There is a blanket and pillow as well. Our team will be on watch tonight so that your team can sleep. It's what we do for each other."

Richard nodded, knowing that he would have done the same if Abe had been the one in his position.

Early the next morning, Chani slipped into a seat in Richard's vehicle, watching as Timothy did the same. He looked better that morning, she decided, before she turned to look out of the window. It was still dark. She could not understand leaving at that time of the morning. She would have thought that daylight would be better. She frowned as she saw vehicles moving in around their vehicle.

Richard had been watching her, guessing at her thoughts.

"We have company back to your town, Chani. It's a given that they know that you two got away and they'll be looking for you. This way, we get you home safe."

Chani nodded, her eyes closing as she prayed. This time, her abduction had scared her as much as it had terrified her. She had not been able to speak with Timothy while they were held captive. He had spent a lot of the time sleeping, worrying her that he had been badly injured.

Ronan looked up as he heard the door to Richard's house open and multiple footsteps. He heard the surprised cry from Eilis and then was on his feet, heading for the living room. His steps stopped as he saw Timothy, unsteady as he was on his feet. Then, he felt a body hit him and arms wrapping around him. Chani had found him.

Chani wrapped her arms as tight as she could around Ronan, desperate to feel safe and treasured. Her tears soaked into his flannel shirt and she felt his kiss on the top of her head.

"Chani? What? Where did you come from?" Ronan finally found his voice.

"Abe and Richard found us. Last night. They wouldn't bring us home last night. Instead, they had us up at some unearthly hour of the morning, put us in a convoy or caravan, and brought us home." She was grumbling, she knew, but she could hear Richard and his team laughing.

"They did, did they? Richard, thank you. What can you tell us?"

"I need food." Chani moved away, heading for her aunt and her hug before moving past her into the kitchen. "They didn't let us eat before we were on the road. That's not right."

Richard continued to laugh even as his hand went out to steady Timothy. Timothy would be seeing someone that day for a physical assessment. But for now, he would be off on sick leave. Don stood beside Richard, watching closely. He didn't know Chani so to have her react that way had been a surprise.

———

"Surprised you, Don?" Silver paused as she walked by. "That's Chani. She's one of a kind but we love her."

Ronan broke up into laughter at that, knowing Silver had done that deliberately. He could hear Chani's protest and then her family's voices telling her it was true.

"Richard?" Ronan paused once more.

"We'll talk, Ronan. I need to find Frank and then I'll be back. Both Don's team and mine will be here for now. That's not up for discussion."

"I gathered that. I do need to go home, though, to do my chores." Ronan was not backing down, not any more.

Chapter 37

Ronan moved around his barn, tidying it up, ensuring that his cattle were taken care of. There was really little that needed to be done, but he had wanted to be there. He wanted to be with Chani but Frank had appeared, simply shaking his head at Ronan. He had to speak with Chani, he seemed to be saying.

Ian approached Ronan, laying a hand on his son's arm.

"Ronan? Talk to me. What is going on?"

"Chani's back." He blinked as he heard words of praise from his father. "Abe and Richard found them last night. She's fine, I think. I haven't had a chance to speak with her. Frank moved in."

"He'll need that time with her, Ronan. Come with me, son. Let Mom and I pray with you."

Ronan hung his jacket on a hook, hearing Stephen speaking with Meg before his steps sounded as he walked away. Not sure what his parents wanted, Ronan sat, taking with thanks the mug of coffee his mother handed him. She sat beside him, his father across from him. He waited, knowing that one of them would speak when they were ready. He was not surprised when his father began to pray.

Looking up thirty minutes later, Ronan sipped at his coffee, his eyes shifting between his parents. They were watching one another, silent communication going on between them.

"Son, your mother and I are proud of the man you have become. You serve God wherever He has put you. That being said, this is a difficult time for you. It is never easy to face danger. We know that only too well. We have faced that when we have been overseas, as you know. But nothing we faced has been like this."

Ronan nodded, knowing that his father had spoken the truth but knowing that he had more to say.

"What your father is trying to say, Ronan, is that while we are proud of you as a man, but as a Christian and follower of Christ, you are an example to all of us. Even with this, your faith has been shaken and tried but you still have stood firm. So has the lady who you have chosen. You don't need to tell us that, we can see how much you love her. We welcome her into our family." His mother brushed tears from her cheeks before she reached for a small jewelry box. "This was your maternal grandmother's ring. She asked that we give it to you when you had found your lady. It was okay with her if it wasn't your first choice but she still wanted your lady to have something that meant a lot to her. She would have loved Chani. They are so much alike."

Ronan grinned at that, thinking of his maternal grandmother. She had been a feisty lady who was not afraid to call things as she saw them but she had been a prayer warrior for the family and their church. She was missed very much, he knew.

"Thank you, Mom. Dad. I don't know where Chani and I are heading, but I do love her. And she loves me. We need to get through this first. And that doesn't seem to be happening. I mean we did come up with a name."

"The name, son?" Ian paled as he heard it. "Him? Of course. He's always had it in for you. He has been prevented many times from harming you. I just found that out yesterday when I was speaking with Garrett. I don't know how he determined that but he has."

"Why, Dad? I don't understand."

"I don't know the full story, but he has been jealous of you since you were young. We kept you apart as much as we could. The schools worked with us as well. That was before he was removed and sent to a private school. I heard that he resented that and blamed you. Now, I'm not saying that is why he is acting like this, but it is likely a part of it."

"But where does Chani come in? Or does she?"

"She does but not how you think. As far as we can determine, she has had no contact with him. Not until that day you showed up at the office and you were both abducted. He was following you for some reason and took the opportunity to take both of you. We are still working through why."

"He's not working on his own. He doesn't have the smarts for that. Where does he work?"

"That's the thing, Ronan." Ronan turned to face his mother, seeing how disturbed she was. "He doesn't seem to work. And we have heard that his parents kicked him out of the house. He's been living on the streets and moving from house to house. He can't keep a job. His anger gets in the way."

"I can see that as well." Ronan grew quiet, thinking back over the years and his contact with the man. "I know who is behind him." His eyes slid shut. "It's not who you would ever expect."

"Who, Ronan?" Richard had appeared, sitting quietly beside Ronan.

"His uncle on his father's side. He has always been involved in crime. We knew that as kids. If you wanted anything on the black market, you went to him. If you wanted drugs or alcohol as a minor, that's who you approached. Complaints were made over the years, but he never faced arrest or any consequences. Would that change things for us if he had?"

Richard shook his head, knowing the man who Ronan had named. Ronan was correct in his assumption. Somehow, this man had bought off someone to keep himself out of jail. They just had to find that person. Then maybe this would be over for Ronan and Chani.

"Ronan, Chani mentioned that she was sent her mother's music box. How did that happen?" Meg watched her son closely.

"I don't know, Mom. They don't either. Chani doesn't remember seeing it when they cleared out the house. Her sister, cousins, and aunt don't either. That means it was gone before they did that. But what else is missing that will show up unexpectedly?"

"That's a good question, son. We will pray for that to be resolved." Ian shared a look with Richard, both of the men with similar thoughts. They knew that there were still two young ladies to face difficulties and what this meant with the gloves and music box might not be solved until it came to Ashlynn.

Richard excused himself as he felt his phone vibrating and walked outside, finding Stephen waiting for him.

"Stephen? Talk to me. What did you find?"

"This." Stephen's face was grim as he held up a small box. "It was on Ronan's truck. His truck has not moved for a few days from what I can remember. Whoever left it knew that Ronan was not around. I've a call into his security company, but they said that the feed was down this morning, early, for a few moments."

"That's when that happened then. How do we even keep them safe?"

Chapter 38

Ronan walked back from his barn that night. He knew his parents were around somewhere, in town, if he remembered correctly. Silver was around, likely preparing a meal for them. He sighed. This was not how he had planned tonight. Not at all. He had wanted to find Chani, ask her that question that was hovering on his lips and then see if his grandmother's ring would do. Only, she wasn't around. She had disappeared once more, not one person knowing where she was.

He turned as he heard a slight noise, a frown on his face as he saw a man approaching. He relaxed when he recognized him.

"Simon? You're at my place?" He reached to shake Simon's hand.

"I am, Ronan. The young lady inside told me where to find you." Simon was puzzled.

"Security, Simon. I have a security team with me. Silver is here for just a bit longer and then one of the men moves in. Mom and Dad are around too."

"I met Silver. Now, what can we do for you?" Simon watched his young friend carefully, seeing that he had healed from one assault but not this latest one.

"For me? I'm not sure that I understand." Ronan held the back door for Simon before he shed his boots and jacket.

Simon nodded his thanks at Silver as she pointed to the table. She had set out their meal, leaving Ian and

Meg's share in the oven. She moved away, reaching for her jacket and heading outside.

"For you. John has been concerned about you. Frankie has been as well. They thought that maybe a retired lawyer might be able to help you."

Ronan paused as he reached for his fork, bowing his head to ask the blessing on their food. He thought through what they had discovered and nodded. Simon would help. He didn't know the town, the people, and might just see a connection. He turned his head as he heard the door open. Richard appeared, nodding at the two men before he grabbed a cup of coffee and sat with them.

"Richard, Simon here has offered to help go over everything. He's the one who found me all that time ago." Ronan continued to eat, his mind on what they had discovered. He stood suddenly, excused himself and headed for his office.

Simon turned on his chair to watch him, not seeing the look that Richard had shot after Ronan.

"He's discovered something." Simon's voice was quiet but certain in his words.

"He has. And that means he's going to go out there, doesn't it?" Richard was on his feet, following Ronan. "Ronan?"

Ronan's finger was in the air, stopping Richard's words. Simon simply wandered the room, studying the papers that had been transferred from Richard's home to Ronan's. He paused at one sheet, a frown on his face before he turned. He found Richard beside him, his eyes on the names.

"Simon?" Richard shifted so that he could watch Ronan, finding Ronan watching Simon.

Ronan was on his feet, standing beside Simon, his eyes on the paper

"Him. He's been a thorn in my side for years. No, he's not a friend. He's someone I try to avoid at all costs. And he is cousin to Ryan."

"That's your connection. He has been arrested in Riverville over the last week. Frankie said he would be reaching out to your force." Simon looked around. "Now, how do we find out more about him?"

"We don't, Simon. We work with what we have here." Richard sighed as Ronan pointed to his computer and directed Simon there. No, he thought, they'll work on their own. He walked away, heading for the outside and the team who was waiting. He needed all of them there for now.

Simon looked up as he heard other voices, standing to greet Ian and Meg. He realized that he knew them from conferences at their churches.

"Simon? You're here?" Meg turned to Ronan. "And just what are you two up to?"

"We found another name, Mom. A cousin of Ryan's. Now, Simon has been working away. He has found information that we have asked Evan and Emma to verify. They're working on that. Emma has said that she was reaching out to Frank."

"That's good. Now, what can we do?" Ian stood with an arm around his son's shoulder.

"We need to compile all that we have into a neat package. That's your task, Dad. Mom, we'll be working overnight by the looks of it." Ronan turned to his mother, finding her nodding.

"Not a problem, son. I can provide food and coffee. That's my task." Meg turned to walk away, finding Ashlynn standing in the hallway. "Ashlynn?"

"The girls and I have arrived. Gareth is working with his father and will be here shortly. We've stepped back from our work for now. That is, except for Gareth. Garrett said he had material to bring as well."

"That's good. Now, the girls?"

"They're bringing in what we need from the cars. Then, they will work with the men. We want this solved and solved now."

"So do we. And I think that we will. Now, what can we prepare for meals?"

"We brought bread and sandwich stuff. Brinn picked up salad stuff and veggies. Darbi brought fruit. Eilis reached out to the church, asking that the prayer line work overnight for us."

"That does help. How do people who have no faith get through times like this?" Meg turned and greeted the girls, taking what they had brought. She raised her eyes to find Frank walking in behind them, a grim smile on his face.

Chapter 39

Dawn was breaking as Ronan rose, stretched, and yawned. They had been working overnight, finding information that they passed on to Frank. Frank had worked away with them as well, leaving shortly before to head to the office. He felt he had enough information to start looking at search warrants and arrest warrants. Ronan appreciated that Frank had been willing to go that extra mile. It had not surprised him.

Walking towards his barn, Ronan stared up at the sky, watching as dawn broke in rosy colours on the eastern horizon. He felt that today was the day, the day that he found his lady love, and brought her home. How he was that confident? He could not say. He only knew that today would bring about danger and answers.

Timothy approached him, just standing with him for a moment without saying anything. Richard had been in and out of the house overnight, returning each time to brief his team. Don and his team had moved in as well, each one deeply concerned that Ronan's life was at stake. That was the rumbling on the streets, that Ronan was to die and that Chani would disappear somewhere.

"Ronan? Let's get you out of sight." Timothy pointed to the barn. "I'll help you this morning. We have people around here but they can still get through, even to bringing in a sniper."

Ronan paled at that.

"A sniper? What are you saying, Timothy?" Ronan walked towards the barn, reaching to pull open the door and turn on lights.

"That the word on the street is that you are to die." Timothy watched Ronan closely, trying to judge his response.

"I see." Ronan walked away, heading for his first chore of the morning. "They can try, Timothy, but God has ultimate control. I will not die unless He has decided that it is my turn to do so. Now, what do we do today?'

"We get you through these chores. And then you get some sleep. You'll need it." Timothy worked away with Ronan, content for the moment that Ronan was safe.

Ronan roused early that afternoon. He had stretched out on a couch, asleep as soon as he laid his head on a pillow. His mother had stood beside him, assessing him, before she reached to cover him, her hand resting on his hair. He wasn't sure what had awakened him, but he could hear the conversation swirling through his house. On his feet, he finger combed his hair into place and headed for a mug of coffee. He found Frank handing him one before he pointed Ronan to a chair.

"Frank? What has happened? I know something has." Ronan refused to back down, knowing that Frank had information and he wanted that information.

Frank's head dropped as he prayed. Yes, he did have information but he wasn't at liberty to share it all.

"Something has, Ronan. We have discovered more information, thanks to what you all have done. We have narrowed our search and are planning on moving into that building shortly." He watched with compassion as Ronan's eyes slid closed.

"Is she there?" Ronan's voice was barely above a whisper. "Is Chani there?"

"We think so. That is what the word is." Frank's hand on his arm kept Ronan in his chair. "This is when it gets very dangerous for you. We need you to stay here. Don and Richard are pulling their teams in tight to you. Whoever this is will not go after her family or yours. They want you."

"It's been me all along, hasn't it?" Ronan blinked to clear his eyes, his mind racing. "I still don't get it."

"We're working through all that, Ronan. We have been working up the chain of command. It goes much deeper than what you think. Much deeper and darker. We'll explain it all. But for now, our focus is finding Chani and keeping you safe in the meantime."

Ronan nodded, his thoughts on his lady. His prayers were deeper and wider than they had been. He had had to come to the conclusion that she might not come home as he wished, that they might have to have a funeral for her. He had released her and felt peace about that. God was working in his life, he knew, but he wished that there had been a different way for that to have happened.

"I see, Frank. That's okay. I'll stay safe." Ronan was on his feet, heading for the stairs and to his bedroom, seeking a shower, shave, and clean clothes. He felt he needed to be ready to greet his lady love, that she would be home that very day.

Frank watched him walk away before he reached for their mugs, rinsing them out and setting them in the sink. He sighed. This was where he always hesitated in an investigation. He had to make sure that he had all the information that was required, but something inside him told him that one little piece was missing. He walked back through Ronan's office, searching the walls before he nodded. He tapped at a name, knowing that was who they needed to find.

Richard watched Frank walk away before he headed to the paper that Frank had stopped at. His surprise was quickly hidden. Of course, he thought. That person. Ronan and Chani were in more danger than they all thought. And just how they were to save them was a large question that he had no answer for.

Silver approached, her eyes on Richard. Something had just changed, she knew, but also knew that Richard would think it through and then discuss it with them.

"Richard?" Silver's voice broke into Richard's thoughts.

"Silver? Where are the rest of the team?"

"Grabbing something to eat. Don sent us in. Then, he'll split his team to eat. What just happened?"

Richard's finger tapped at the paper just as Frank's had done.

"This happened. They had the name all along. Only, we didn't know that. Now, we have to plan."

Silver paled as she read the name. Richard was right. It had been there all along. And now she felt like they would be running a marathon to catch up. *Emma, this would be a good time for you to come through,* she thought. *We need your research.*

Chapter 40

The day that she disappeared once more, Chani had struggled as she was pulled from the vehicle, not liking the feel of the man's hands on her. She stared at the house, shock on her face. This place? It can't be right, she thought. There is no way that they would be involved.

Shoved inside and to an interior room, Chani stumbled over her feet and went down hard on her hands and knees. She heard the door close behind her. She waited and then reached for the gag, pulling it from her face and wiping her arm across her mouth. There was a bad taste in her mouth from it.

Searching the room, Chani found the small ensuite and turned on the taps. Her mouth was rinsed out repeatedly as she tried to get rid of the taste. Drying her face, she turned to stare into the room before moving rapidly around it. There was no way out, she saw. No windows to jump from. The door was locked. A prisoner once more, she decided. Only she was not going to be some meek, docile prisoner. Not at all. She was ready for a fight and fight she would. God was there with her, she knew. She needed the strength and courage that came from Him.

Hours passed or so it seemed to her as she thought about it later. The door had opened briefly, only long enough for a tray to be set down on the table by the door. She couldn't get a good look at the man, he had kept his face turned away from her.

The next morning, the door opened, and a man appeared. Chani drew in a deep breath. She knew him, knew his reputation, and didn't have a good feeling about what she faced. Her prayer was rush and urgent. She did not feel safe around him, not at all.

"Well, Chani. You are in my hands. I will not let you go, not at all. Your boyfriend will come to terms and do what I want. Even if he does, he'll never see you again."

Adam Gray sneered at her. His son, Ryan, had been one that they had determined to be involved.

"I don't think so. I have no idea what you want or need. And Ronan is not my boyfriend."

"Sure he is. We've watched you two."

"No, he's not. He's a friend. That's all. So, if you are finished, I would like to leave and leave now." Chani walked towards him, forcing him back towards the door. She wasn't quite quick enough to make it out before the door was slammed shut and locked.

Chani stared at the door, unable to believe that it was locked again. She carefully turned the knob, finding it to be true. She would not be getting out of there, not any time soon. Her forehead rested against the door. This was not the result that she had planned on. Not at all. Her plan had been to walk right by him and out of the door to freedom.

Hours passed, with no one coming around her. She sighed to herself at last, looking down at her watch. It was late evening, she saw, and that worried her. No one had brought her a meal and she was ravenous. Being hungry made her grumpy. And being grumpy made her angry. It always had. It was something that she was working on but it didn't help in this situation. She could only pray for her family and for Ronan and his family.

Chani finally slept, unable to stay awake. She didn't hear the door open and the man appear once more. He stared at her in anger, wanting her awake but willing to wait. She wasn't going anywhere, he thought.

Chani roused once more, her senses letting her know that someone had been in the room. She was now scared, frightened, terrified. Her anger had changed to that. She didn't like that feeling. She was on her feet, searching for a way out, pushing at the door without any results.

Gray listened to her footsteps from where he stood outside the door. He gave an evil grin, knowing that her imprisonment was working on her mind. Give her enough time, he thought, and she would be putty in his hands. It wasn't just revenge and retribution against Ronan that he wanted. He wanted the same for her. Only he would not admit that to anyone.

Chani dropped to the floor, hiding her face against her upraised knees. She was desperate to get away, but there wasn't any chance for her to get away. *God, where are You? Don't You even care? I need to get away but I can't. Please protect and comfort my family and my love.*

Chani roamed the room, restless, unable to settle down. She would drop into the upholstered easy chair for a bit and then rise to pace. She would drop down on the bed and try to sleep. Only sleep never came. She was under too much tension to do just that.

Late that night, Chani slept at last. She didn't hear the shouts and gunfire that sounded outside of the house. The unlocking of the door startled her and had her on her feet. She was on her feet, backing away as Gray approached her.

"You're coming with me. And no fighting." His hand gripped her in a hard, hurting manner as he dragged her from the room and to the back of the house. He shoved open a door, a gun in his hand. She was pulled roughly from the house and then towards the woods behind it. She could hear yells from behind her. Chani struggled as hard as she could, tugging at her arm, her free hand clawing at his hand. She just wasn't able to free herself.

Frank stood in the open doorway to the room, anger on his face. They were too late, he thought. He just couldn't figure out where Chani was. He spun as his name was called and he ran for the outside.

"He got by us somehow, Frank." The patrol officer was angry. "How did that happen?"

"Which way?" Frank spun in a circle, not seeing anyone other than law enforcement.

"Frank! This way!"

Frank spun once more, then ran for the officer heading his way.

"What do you have?"

"Footprints. A man and a woman. They're heading for the buildings at the back of the lot."

Frank headed that way, praying that he would be in time. Only, he didn't think that he would be. He stood in the open doorway, frustration and fear evident. Gray had escaped and taken Chani with him. Now, they had to go through this all over again, searching for him and praying that they found him before something dire happened to Chani.

Chapter 41

Frank walked back into his office, fatigue dogging each step he took. They had failed to find Chani, even though each man and woman had tried their best. He knew that interviews were going on right then, each investigator doing their best to find Chani. Only, it didn't seem as if that would work.

He sighed heavily as he reached for the pot of coffee in the break room, not caring that it was old. His head dropped for a moment before he turned, mug of coffee in hand, and headed back to his office. Frank was not leaving there until he had some answers. That would be difficult to do, he knew, but that was his goal.

Reaching for his phone, he retrieved his voice mail messages. He hesitated as he heard the one from Ashlynn and then the one from Ronan. Somehow, both of them had determined that Chani was still a captive and still in danger. They had both simply stated that they were praying for Frank and his team.

Looking up three hours later, Frank waved an investigator into his office. He reached for the piece of paper that he was handing, his eyes not leaving the woman's face. He was on his feet, reaching for his coat.

"We have search warrants for this address?"

"We do. I walked over myself and got them." She held them up for him. "Let's go find him, Frank. We need to get Chani safe and home to her family."

———

Frank watched the hangar at the local airport closely. They had confirmed that Gray was there. A flight plan had been filed for himself and a passenger. An informant had confirmed that it was a woman. And the only woman that Frank could think of was Chani.

The officers moved in quietly, approaching Gray as he stood in the guest area of the airport. He turned as he heard their footsteps, a sneer on his face.

"What are you doing here? This is a private area." He turned to walk away but Frank's voice and words stopped him.

"You are under arrest, Gray. For multiple causes but for starters, kidnapping." Frank walked up to him, slapping the arrest warrant at Gray's chest. "Cuff him and take him in." He walked over to the pilot. "He's not going anywhere today. Now, there is a woman listed. Where is she?"

"He's waiting for her. It's his wife." The pilot had paled, knowing that he was now involved in something that he had no desire to be involved in.

Frank nodded, turning as he heard the strident voice of a woman and watched as she was handcuffed and led away. He sighed. Chani wasn't here and hadn't been. Now came the search for her. He felt uneasy, knowing that Gray could have killed her already.

One of the officers approached him, worried about something. Frank waited for him to speak

"Chani? She's not here. Where is she?"

“We need to track his trail from his house to here at the airport. That’s going to be difficult.” Frank walked away and then spun, walking back, a hand on the officer’s arm. “He had a driver?”

“He did.” The officer’s face lit up. “I’ll track him down and bring him in. He’s an accessory right now. He may squeal on him to lighten his own sentence.”

Frank watched from behind the two-way mirror as an investigator dropped a file folder on a table in an interrogation room. Gray’s driver sat there, a sneer on his face. It was obvious that he had no intention of cooperating.

Frank watched as documents were produced by the investigator. He could not hear the conversation but saw the driver’s demeanour begin to change. He lost his arrogance bit by bit before he dropped his head in surrender. Frank watched as the investigator made notes and then rose, opening the door and motioning for an officer. The driver was handcuffed and led away. Defeat showed in how he moved and stood.

Moving to the hallway, Frank waited for the investigator to return.

“Frank? He gave us a list of places where they stopped. He did give details of a place where Chani disappeared with Gray. He has no idea if she is alive or dead. I’m working on a search warrant so that we can go in.”

“Good work. Find me when you get it. I want in on this. In the meantime, I have some calls to make.”

Frank sat back at last in his desk chair. He was still awaiting word that the warrant was ready. Emma had called, simply stating that she had word of where Chani was. That address was one that the driver had given them. He had thanked Emma, listening as she gave a number of names who were involved. He had no idea how she did it, but she had confirmed what they had been looking at.

Frank watched the building closely. It was a ramshackle house, almost falling down. He wasn't sure that they could even get in or out before it completely collapsed.

"How do you want to work it, Frank?" The officer stood beside him, the investigator on the other side.

"Three of us go in. That way, we're not causing too much stress on the structure. Us three. The others stay out here and watch. We have paramedics here?"

"We do. They would move in when we need them."

Frank shook his head, looking around, seeing the paramedics standing nearby.

"We can't risk it. We go in, find Chani, and then bring her out. I don't see any other way of doing it."

"You're right, Frank. That's how we'll work it." The investigator turned, holding out the search warrant to another officer. "Hold on to this. Serve it if someone shows up."

The three men walked forward, stepping carefully. Frank paused at the entrance, saying a prayer for their safety and to find Chani before he snapped on the large flashlight that he carried and stepped forward. The light swept the rooms, seeing the debris that had piled up. He brought the light back to a certain spot as the officer gave a sound and moved towards the debris. Frank watched as the officer dropped to his knees and then looked up, nodding. The officer stood, Chani gathered close in his arms. The only thing was that she was not moving or alert.

Chapter 42

Frank jumped up to sit in a corner of the paramedic rig, his eyes on Chani. She had not roused and that concerned him very much. The paramedic, Stu by name, shook his head at Frank.

"What happened to her, Frank?"

"We don't know. She had been abducted and then dumped here. What can you tell me?"

"Not a lot. She's alive but not by much. It's as if she was given an overdose." The paramedic was suddenly searching Chani's arms, pushing the sleeves back before he pointed. "There is nothing showing a needle mark. But she does have bruising around her temple." His motions were still hurried as he monitored her vitals, started the IV, and shoved an oxygen mask on her face.

"Are we in time?" Frank could barely ask his question. He had no desire to explain to Chani's family and friends that they had found her but not in time.

"I think so. Whoever did this really didn't care what happened to her. She's very cold and that is shutting down her system." He squinted through the window, watching as the rig backed up to the ambulance entrance at the hospital. "We'll get her into more treatment."

Frank paced outside the examination room, worried about Chani. He turned his phone over and over, knowing that he had to call Ashlynn and Ronan but afraid that they would arrive too late. He walked away to a corner where he could stand and watch the room door but where it was a little quieter.

"Ashlynn?" Frank could hear conversation in the background as Ashlynn answered her phone. "Where are you?"

"Still at Ronan's. We're trying to come up with a place for you. Do you have news?" Ashlynn's arm was around Eilis as she crowded close to her aunt.

"I do. We have her." Frank had to stop speaking as he heard the sobs coming from his friend. "Ashlynn, we have her. She's been hurt and is in the hospital. Have Richard and Don bring you all in."

"We'll do that. Praise God! She's back. And thank you, Frank." Ashlynn turned as Brinn and Darbi approached her, hugging each one. She turned to find Ronan standing close, hope on his face.

"Ashlynn? Frank has her? Is she okay?" He could barely speak through the tears choking his throat. Ashlynn reached to hug him, finding Meg beside her to do the same.

"He has her. He hasn't said much other than that she is in the hospital." She turned as she felt a hand on her arm. "Richard?"

"We'll sort you out but right now, we need to pray." Richard was as good as his word, praying for Chani and her family, followed by Don, Ian and Garrett. Gareth had had to leave, but Brinn quickly sent off a text message to him.

Sorting themselves out into vehicles, Ashlynn stared out into the darkness. She still felt a heaviness of concern about Chani, knowing that Frank had not said everything that he could or would. That information he would rather say in person, she knew.

Frank walked towards them as they milled around in the waiting room.. He had just spoken with the physician, and the news was better than he had thought. Chani was rousing but still not out of the woods. That would come with time and treatment.

"Frank?" Ashlynn stopped short, her worried eyes on him.

"It's okay, Ashlynn. She's rousing. I can't go into too many details. The physician will let you know what happened. She was removed from where she had been kept and moved to another location." Frank spoke with them for a little while longer before he walked away. He paused, fatigue drawing his strength as he stood, his eyes on the stars. *Thank you, Father. She is safe but we still need to finish off this investigation. We still don't have everyone.*

Ashlynn stood an hour later, an arm around Eilis, and watched as Chani slept. She would be staying overnight for observation, much to her protest. She had complained and then slept. Darbi and Brinn had been in and then left, heading for home. Ashlynn had sent them that way. She sighed. Ronan had refused to leave, simply stating that he needed to be there. Chani needed him. None of them could deny that. They were two parts of a whole, they all knew.

Richard was still around, Don and his team leaving. They had to be out of town the next day for an assignment. Richard had promised to keep Don up to date on what was going on.

The physician paused as the nurse approached, his eyes on Chani. She was chilled through and through. X-rays had not shown anything, but he knew that she had been abused. The wound on her head had been cleaned and treated.

"Her family is here."

Paul Wilson nodded. He knew Ashlynn from church but didn't know the girls as well.

"I will be out shortly. She's starting to warm up but it will take time. We need to find whoever did this."

"We do, Paul." Merrylee turned. "I'll let them know that you will be out shortly." She paused, not sure how to continue.

"What is it, Merrylee?" Paul turned slightly to watch her.

"Ronan is out there. I know him from school. I don't understand why he would be."

"They were involved in something together. That was my understanding. Although I have seen Ronan and Chani together lately."

Merrylee nodded, knowing that Paul likely was correct.

Ashlynn looked up at last, finding Frank in front of her. She patted the seat beside her, watching closely as Frank hesitated and sat.

"You found her, Frank. For now, that is all that concerns us. I know that you have information that you need to confirm, people to interrogate. We get that. All that we are concerned about right now? That's Chani."

"Have you been back yet?" Frank watched the three girls, seeing them huddling together. Gareth was seated beside Ronan, Ronan's parents beside him.

"We have. She's rousing but Paul said it would be a while. They're trying to warm her up."

"And they will. God is not ready for her to come home yet." Frank's head rested against the wall as his eyes closed. He was exhausted, deep to the bone exhausted, but his day was not over. He needed to head back to the office and the investigation.

Chapter 43

Her eyes flickering open and closed, Chani snuggled down under the covers. She was warm, she thought, and really didn't care where she was. That was all that mattered. The last that she could barely remember was feeling very cold and not wanting to move. She felt a hand on hers before she slept.

Ronan watched as Chani tried to wake up, sighing to himself as she slept. She needed that, he knew, but he needed her to wake up. He reached to drop a kiss on her cheek before he walked away. His time with her was up. There were others waiting for her.

The nurse watched Ronan head for the waiting room and into his mother's hug. His father stood beside them, his arms around his family. Praying for them, the nurse decided, before she headed to her tasks. Chani was rousing and would likely go home that day.

Two hours later, Ashlynn walked into Chani's room, finding her sitting up, Eilis beside her on the bed. The other two girls were seated on the foot of it.

"Aunt Ash? Where have you been?" Chani reached to hug her aunt. "The doctor says that I can go home if my blood work is okay. It's been too long that I have been in here."

"Not that long, Chani. Has Frank been around?"

Chani gave a disgruntled sound, her brows lowered.

"He was. He picked my brain of just about everything that I know." She frowned even harder as the four ladies laughed. "It's not funny."

"No, it's not but you are." Ashlynn stood back, feeling an arm around her shoulder. Ronan had approached, listening to Chani. "We'll take you home, Chani." Ashlynn's hand went up. "You will come back to my place or to one of the girls. There will be no discussion about that."

Chani slowly nodded, her eyes finding Ronan's. She sighed to herself. And Ronan was here, she thought. Here to try and protect. Only that's not possible. She remembered the words spewed at her in anger before the blow had landed on her head. She didn't remember much after that, except that she had felt chilled and then nothing.

Ronan dropped to a seat beside Chani late that afternoon. She had curled up under a blanket, a pillow stuffed between herself and the end of the couch. He reached for her hand, rubbing her fingers. Hers tightened on his.

"Chani? Can you talk about what happened?" His voice was low, barely audible.

Chani slowly nodded, not wanting to speak but knowing that she had to.

"I can. We don't have the head one yet. Frank knows that. Gray wasn't him or her even though he tried to portray that he was."

"I didn't think that he was. Richard was working on something, heading out for somewhere." Ronan tilted his head to watch her. "I love you, Chani. I was so worried about you."

Chani nodded before she shot a glance towards the kitchen. For once, she and Ronan were alone.

"I love you too, Ronan. I thought that I would never see you again." She leaned against him before his arm was around her.

"How do we figure out who is in charge?" Ronan's voice was still quiet, his eyes on Garrett as he approached.

"We've found that person, Chani. Ronan. At least, we have the name. We just have to find them. They're hiding." Garret sat, dropping a folder onto the coffee table.

"I know who it is." Chani blinked back tears. She said a name, causing Ronan to stare at her in shock, Garrett to simply nod.

"That's who is it, Chani. Someone we have all trusted. Frank is aware of the name. I just spoke with him. Apparently, Evan and Shea were suspicious and did some digging."

"How long?" Chani could barely get the words out. "He almost killed me through Gray. And I don't understand why."

"None of us do. Not at this point. Frank has been told to go home and get some sleep. He hasn't been out of the office for over forty-eight hours." Garrett sat back, watching the younger couple. He had to talk to them but right now was not the time. He rose, pointing to the folder. "Look through that. Then talk to me." He walked away, leaving Chani staring at the folder and Ronan staring at Chani.

"Chani? What are you thinking?" Ronan spoke at last, his eyes on Eilis as she approached them, a tray in her hands. "Thank you, Eilis."

Chani shuddered for a moment, remembering the venom spewed at her that day. She had just been driven around and then to that building. Forced to walk inside, her shoes had been ripped from her feet. She had begged to be let go. She wouldn't talk, she promised. All to no avail, it seemed. She rubbed at her head, feeling once more the blow that had landed and sent her spiralling down into darkness and to the floor

"I don't know, Ronan. I mean, I think it's him but I still think there is something else. Something tied to Mom and Dad that we have not yet figured out."

"I know there is, sis. But what?" Eilis reached for the folder, curiosity getting the better. She opened it, surprised at whose picture was there. "Chani? Did you see this?"

Chani shook her head, reaching for it. Ronan leaned over to study the photo.

"That's the head person, Chani. Even above the one who you named."

"I know. I have always felt evil around them. Now, how do we prove it?"

"We don't." Ronan handed Eilis back the folder and then simply hugged Chani, missing the speculative look that they were given.

"But we will, Ronan. Don't you see? They won't stop until I am dead or you are." Chani rubbed at her face, willing the tears back down. Fear was moving through her, a stronger fear than she had ever felt in her life.

Chapter 44

Two days later, Chani stood in the parking lot at the church, her arms wrapped around herself. Ronan stood behind her, his arms around her, holding her tight to him. They had arrived for their usual Bible study, both needing that. However, they had never made it into the building. They had been stopped by a couple, a couple that Chani was afraid to face. Only, she didn't seem to have much choice in the matter. Ronan could feel the simmering anger in her and see it on her face.

"Chani? Are you coming?" Eilis approached, her steps slowing as she saw Chani just standing there. "Chani?" Her eyes moved from her sister to Ronan and then to the couple. She drew in a deep breath. This is not what is needed, she thought. Not at this point and not them.

"Go on in, Eilis. I will be in shortly. This won't take long." Chani didn't look at her sister, merely nodded towards the church.

Eilis started to move away, stopping as she felt a hand on her arm. This is not good, she thought again. The couple's son had moved in and stopped Eilis from leaving. She felt for her phone in her pocket, hoping to be able to call for help before something awful happened.

Chani stiffened her knees. Her legs were shaking with fear. Ronan's arms helped keep her upright. She had not expected to face that couple out here. She could see his other son behind them. She knew that Eilis was stopped from moving away. Just how she was to get them out of there, she had no idea, but she would come up with something. She was just afraid that someone would be hurt, and that someone may well belong to her family.

"You're not going anywhere, none of you." Paula Gray spoke, a sneer in her voice and on her face. "You're leaving with us." She looked towards her husband, Joe, who was nodding.

"Just for the record, Paula. What are you involved in?" Chani asked her question, her eyes on Paula but seeing movement around them. She just wasn't sure what all was going on but she prayed that they were friends that were there and not enemies.

Ashlynn had been approaching Chani when Brinn stopped her, Gareth reaching to draw both ladies back from view.

"Brinn? Chani's out there. I need to speak with her." Ashlynn was puzzled, turning to face her niece, finding Brinn watching Chani. "Brinn? Gareth?"

"Chani's in trouble, Aunt Ash. And I don't know that we'll have time to get officers here. Is Frank and his wife here tonight?"

"They are. They're already inside." Ashlynn drew in a deep breath. "It's them, isn't it? I didn't expect them. Not at all." She turned, heading for the church, searching for Frank. "Frank? We need help. The Grays have stopped Chani and Ronan from coming in. Eilis is there as well."

Frank was on his feet, his hand resting on his wife's shoulder.

“Stay here, Ashlynn. I’ll be back.”

Ashlynn opened her mouth to protest but turned as Peg reached to draw her down to the seat that Frank had vacated.

“Stay with me, Ashlynn. Where are to girls?”

“Eilis is with Chani. Brinn was watching with Gareth. Darbi? I have no idea. I hadn’t seen her.” Ashlynn drew in a shuddering breath, barely able to keep her composure. She jumped as she felt an arm around her.

“Aunt Ash? Brinn sent me in to be with you.” Darbi shared a look with Peg. “What’s going on?”

“It’s the Grays. They have stopped Chani, Ronan, and Eilis. I need to be out there.” She started to rise, finding Garrett there as well as Ian. “Garrett? Ian? Don’t tell me!”

“So far, they are okay. Frank has called for help and found the officers who were already here in the church. They’re surrounding them. They’ll keep our kids safe.” Gareth shared a look with Peg, who nodded.

Frank watched closely, seeing the anger in Chani. *Please, Chani,* he begged silently, *don’t do anything foolish. She’ll not hesitate to kill you. She’s done that before. I don’t want to explain to anyone why you died. Not when I am not even sure myself.*

Chani shifted her weight, feeling Ronan moving with her. She was desperate to find a way to get Eilis out of there. Ronan, she knew, would not leave her.

That was a given. It was who he was and was ingrained in his character.

"Okay, Paula. Talk. If you're planning on killing us, and I have no doubt those are your plans, I want to know why. What did I ever do to you?"

"Not to me." Paula sneered at her, not looking around. She didn't see the officers moving in, Frank directly behind her.

Frank nodded at Chani to continue with her words. He was confident that they were close enough to prevent any harm from coming to the three young people. The officers had moved in silently being the Grays, watchful and ready.

"Then who did I offend? Or was it me or someone else? I would really like to know why I suffered, why Ronan suffered, and why our families have suffered. You're supposed to be smart. Show us how smart you really are." Chani did not back down from the look of venom shot at her.

Paula shook her head at her husband.

"Let me handle this."

Joe stared at her before his voice roared at her.

"Not this time. This time? I handle it. You have failed in every attempt you have made. How many do you have to make?" Joe turned his anger towards Chani and Ronan. He couldn't care less that Eilis was there. She was non-consequential in his estimation. If she died too, that would be just too bad.

Chapter 45

Chani listened to the Grays, her eyes tracing past them to watch the officers surrounding them from the rear. Frank's nod caught her attention, and she drew a breath of relief. Now, maybe, they would solve their adventure and stop whatever and whoever it was that they needed to.

"Okay, then, Joe. You tell me why." Ronan spoke for the first time, his eyes on the top of Chani's head. He was afraid that she would try something and end up dead.

"You want to know? Okay, let me tell you." Joe's chest puffed up. He was in control. He had these two right where he wanted them. "It's because of you that my sons couldn't get ahead in life. You kept them back."

"What are you talking about? I don't know your sons." Ronan was truly puzzled, not quite sure what he was hearing.

"Yes, you two. You kept my sons back. They couldn't succeed. They told me that. They told me you complained about them all the time in school. And that you prevented them from getting the jobs that they wanted." Joe's anger was building.

Paula scoffed.

"That's not true, Joe. We've talked about that. They didn't get ahead because of you. And you always blamed these two. I agree with you. They are to blame for all the trouble that we've faced." Paula didn't go

---

any further as she watched Joe's hand raise, a weapon in it.

Joe froze as he felt the cold steel of a weapon touch his ear.

"Stop fooling around. This ends now."

"That is so correct, Joe Gray. It does end now." Frank simply reached past him and took the weapon from him. He stepped back as officers moved in, handcuffing the Grays and leading them away. Frank watched and then turned to the young people in front of him.

Chani had frozen, afraid to move as the Grays were arrested. She simply turned at that point, reaching for her sister, leaving Ronan to step backwards as his knees buckled and he dropped to the ground. Frank walked over to him, a hand resting on his shoulder.

"Did he just say that, Frank?" Ronan was having trouble comprehending what had just happened.

"He did, Ronan, ladies. We'll sort it all out but they were the last of who we were looking for."

Frank stood late that night in Ashlynn's kitchen, listening to the conversation swirling around him. He was exhausted and heading home after he spoke with the group. He turned as he felt someone beside him.

Chani stood there, her eyes on him before she reached to hug him.

"Thank you, Frank. It's taken a lot from you."

"It has, Chani, but at least we have solved it for you." He reached to hug her and then Ronan who had followed her. "Let's find the rest and we'll talk."

Ashlynn pulled Chani into a hug, Eilis on Chani's other side. Ronan stood, leaning against a wall, his eyes not moving from Chani.

"What can you tell us, Frank?" Ashlynn spoke for the group. "Chani told us what was said. We don't understand."

"No, we didn't either. We have searched their home. They do blame you but not for what they said. The evidence shows Ronan, that they wanted your farm. For the land. They wanted to develop it. Only no one would approach you about that. Chani? They were jealous of how well liked you and your family are. Without you knowing it, Jake had taken a client on. Their great-aunt. Alice Teeter."

"Alice? She doesn't seem like them at all. She is just so sweet." Chani paled. "She's talked about her crazy niece and her family. How they want her to go into a home and that they want her money. My helping her with her gardens has kept her there." Chani turned to Ronan, her face whitening. "Is that why? They wanted her land and money?"

"It is, Chani. It is worth a lot and they thought that by forcing her into a senior's home, that they would be able to take it over and sell it. That's not happening. They are not her heirs. That much we know.

"And the Grays that attacked and abducted you? His brother and nephew. They were all part of their plan to take over your land and their aunt's. You kept them from that. That was their revenge on both of you. They wanted you to die, Chani, somewhere you would never be found. And Ronan, they wanted you to suffer by losing Chani."

Frank stayed for a while longer before he walked away. He shrugged deeper into his jacket, his eyes on the sky, watching the clouds. *Thank you, Lord. It's over for Chani and Ronan. Now for them to heal. Help us to help them.*

Ronan walked Chani towards her apartment, her hand tight in his. He was still afraid that something would happen to her. Chani turned, walking into his arms, feeling his hug tight around her.

"It's over, Chani. I am so thankful for that." Ronan looked down at her before he kissed her. "We'll talk later, sweetheart. Get some rest tonight." He stood with a hand against the closed door, hearing the locks snap closed. He was exhausted himself and knew that he would have trouble driving home.

Chani moved through her apartment, heading for a shower and then warm night clothes. She reached for her cup of hot chocolate, choosing to curl up on her couch, a warm blanket wrapped around her. Eilis had wanted to come and stay with her, but she had refused. She needed that time to just decompress and understand what really happened.

The town slept, certain of its inhabitants at peace. But there was still an undercurrent building. Where it would stop, no one knew. No one knew who would be swept into its torrents. Not that night. Not for a while.

Chani was on a search five months later. Ronan had asked her to come out to his farm and she had readily agreed. They had been dating for months. She stood near his vegetable garden, seeing the starting of growth in it. She smiled. She was loved by Ronan and loved him in return. She now wore the ring that had been his grandmother's, a ruby set in a simply setting. She loved it and wanted no other.

Ronan stood and watched his lady, loving her more and more. He walked towards her, wrapping her into a hug.

"Happy, sweetheart?"

"I am, Ronan. I am. And you?" She looked up at him, wondering at his height.

"I am, sweetheart." He kissed her before turning her towards the house. "Our families and friends are here. They want to celebrate with us. I talked to the prosecutor today. We don't have to testify. They all took plea deals."

"They did? Oh, that is such an answer to prayer. I was afraid of facing them again." Chani grew silent. "Alice passed away last night. I will miss her."

"I heard that she had. But there is something else?"

"There is. She considered me family, she said. Her lawyer contacted me. She left me everything. I am glad this happened after they were all jailed."

———

"That is a relief." Ronan looked around his kitchen, happy to find his family, Chani's family, and their friends there. He smiled as he watched little Isaac carrying around the little gray tabby kitten that had shown up on his door step one day. He had visions of his and Chani's children doing just that.

Richard approached Chani, assessing how she was at that point.

"Chani?"

"Richard?" She mimicked his tone before she grinned. "I'm okay. Timothy is okay. Ronan is just fine. We got through this."

"We did, by the grace of God. Now that it's all over, will you continue to work with Jake?"

"I will. I enjoy this work so much. My clients are all so special, each one of them. Ronan is happy with his farm. Life is good."

Richard laughed and moved on, leaving Ashlynn to move in on her niece. She hugged Chani and then turned to face the room. People were leaving, having stayed for hours. The girls had left, promising to get together in the next few days.

"Chani? Are you really okay?"

"I am, Aunt Ash. I am. Finally. I just wish we knew for sure what happened with Mom and Dad, but I doubt that we ever will. Now, we're working on the wedding. We want it soon."

"I know that you do. What is keeping you back? You have your dress. Ronan has the license. All you need to do is set a date. I know you want simple. That we can do." Ashlynn hugged her niece once more, a softly whispered prayer hitting Chani's ears.

Ronan claimed her as he watched the last of the company leave. He was content, holding his lady love.

"I don't want to wait, Chani. What date can we set"

"Soon, Ronan. Very soon. We just need to absorb that we are not under attack anymore and that our attackers are away for many years."

"That they are. I love you, Chani. Don't let anyone ever tell you differently." Ronan walked Chani to her car and waited as she started it.

"I love you too, Ronan. And soon, I won't be driving away from you. I will be coming home to here." Chani reached for his kiss, hesitated and then drove away, watching Ronan in her rearview mirror. God had brought a wonderful, compassionate, caring man into her life, to help her be the light and witness in the world. She needed him and he needed her.

Dear Readers:

Thank you for choosing to read the story of Chani and her Ronan. She is the second of His Ladies with the Lamps. That parable has always resounded with me, that we are to be ready when Christ returns but we also need to be ready to be the light and witness in the world.

Once more, Chani and Ronan have only shared their story as I have written. They never share ahead, these characters of mine. They like to keep the author in suspense. But once more, they came through victorious in their walk with God and in their love for one another.

And yet again, they have dragged in many people from other stories. Abe and Emma and his team's stories are in the *His Guardians* series. Doug and Darci is *The Heart of a Lion*. Tag and Ayron, Shea and Breckon, Evan and Flannery are part of *His Dreamseekers*. Frankie and Deidre's story is part of *The Haven of Rest* series. And Richard and Don and their teams are all part of multiple stories. I am hearing rumblings from both teams that they have stories to tell.

The parable of the wise virgins has always been a favourite of mine. I can remember as a child hearing our pastor at the time preach a sermon on it. That has stuck with me. My father would often mention it. Dad was a carpenter but build furniture for me in his later years. He built me a stand for my keyboard, an organ stand that he called it. It has a high back with a music book rack, a roll top cover, storage on either end. I treasure it because it was something that he designed and created, a one of a kind piece. When he did it, he included some very precious things on it. On the back underneath the keyboard portion are seven pieces of wood. These he said were the seven churches in Revelations. On the top of the book rack, he carefully handcrafted what look like lamp chimneys. There are five. These he told me were the five wise virgins from the parable. Dad spent a lot of time in thought but never talked a lot about what he was discovering in Scripture. When he did, it was something like this. Dad graduated to heaven in 2012, about two and a half years after Mom. They are missed so very much.

May God richly bless your walk with Him. Be the light in the world that He desires us to be.

As I finish this novel, it just five years ago that I fulfilled a dream that only my mother knew about before she graduated to heaven. I set fingers to the keyboard and wrote *The Sparrow*. This started off the travel that I have taken on writing.

Ronna